"Speaking of your immortal souls," the Cappadocian said to young Peregrine and his comrades, "may I point out to you that in the adjacent street yonder there are to be found no less than six churches, all formerly Temples of various Abominations, as well as four chantries, a monastery, ten taverns, fifteen wine-cellars, and twenty-five brothels."

Even Appeldore seemed a trifle dazed. "Twenty-five?" he repeated.

"Twenty-five," the Cappadocian assured him. "Is it not abominable?"

"It is more than abominable. It is superfluous."

Here and there oil-lamps had begun to twinkle. The good smell of supper cooking came wafting through the evening air, along with the thick scent of incense. Hawkers called their wares, the musical bonk-bonk-bonk of wodden bell-boards announced vespers, and, over and above it all, a young woman, obviously dead to all shame, leaned out of a first story window. She had on a very lowcut dress, and she had a cithern in her hands, and she began to strum and sing a love-song.

"Well," said Peregrine, shifting his saddle-bags and hitching up his belt and starting off into the street adjacent, "I guess we'll just have to skip the churches, the chantry, and the monastery."

# PEREGRINE: PRIMUS

by
**Avram Davidson**

**SF**
ace books
A Division of Charter Communications Inc.
A GROSSET & DUNLAP COMPANY
360 Park Avenue South
New York, New York 10010

PEREGRINE: PRIMUS

Copyright © 1971 by Avram Davidson

All rights reserved. No part of this book may be repro-
duced in any form or by any means, except for the inclusion
of brief quotations in a review, without permission in writing
from the publisher.


All characters in this book are fictitious. Any resemblance
to actual persons, living or dead, is purely coincidental.

An ACE Book


*Cover art by Michael Herring*

Published simultaneously in Canada

Printed in U.S.A.

# PART
# 1

The year in which Captain Dragonet, a bluff and good-hearted sea-rover with a harmless (one would think) fancy for young ladies with round bosoms, was murdered by a mercenary named George something-or-other, hired by the Municipality of Joppa (a bargain, if that is what it was, which the Municipality would soon regret and rue), was or should have been famous for another event. Peregrine, youngest son of Paladrine—commonly called Palindrome—Sovereign of Sapodilla, known far and wide as "the last pagan king in lower Europe," said farewell to his father and his father's land.

"Well, Peregrine," said the old man, rubbing his nose and eyes.

"Yes, Dadda," said Peregrine. Not, note, not Prince Peregrine.

The old man delicately took his nose between two fingers and turned his head. And at once turned it back again. "Hey, have you heard this one?" he asked, brightly, though a trifle stuffily: " *'Able was I ere I saw Elba'?*"

"Yes, Dadda."

"Oh," said his father, a bit flattened. "Well. Here you go. Hey? Always a wrench, you know, sending off me bastard sons like this. But so it must be, the will and counsel of our forefathers, as necessary today as it was the day they was uttered, whenever that was, me legitimate sons eating me out of house and home—"

"That's all right, Dadda. Comes as no surprise." A spritely young man, Peregrine, well-made and on the

3

slender side, with complexion tending towards the dark, and with a high color nonetheless in his cheeks.

"You've been issued the full ration, now, hasn't you? Plus," he glanced aside and for the tenth time totted up what he saw before him under the mulberry tree before the castle door, which cast a fine shade and made everything squashy underfoot in the berry season. "One fine riding-mule and two sumpter-mules, item. One chest of fine linens, item. One set of best quality second-rate arms and armor, item. One—"

"It's all there, Dadda. Prince Buddy's mother checked it through three times with the master-list."

His father's eyes and nose were all very red by now, but he fired up at this mention of his wife. "Drat that woman. Afraid you might get a grommet too many, I suppose. Ah well. You're well out of it, lad. This lot is washed up, last me own time, and then, ho! and scrabble for it. Time was," he said, wistfully, tugging at a grey hair in his aft nostril, and waving away some elderly nanny-nurses and thralls who were weeping nearby, "when a petty king like me could always make a decent submission to the Imperial court, get a bang-up banquet and a parade, and retire on a good enough pension and never have to worry about collecting a tax or balancing a bloody budget in your life again. But," he sighed and blew out his pigeon-grey moustachios, "that's all washed up now. Religious bigotry is what's done for that. Treats you like the dirt under their feet, them Christians, is what they does, and that's a fact. Call that Brotherhood? Hahr! And as for turning me coat, for that's what it amounts to, chop and change it as you may, and stripping to the buff and climbing into one of them bloody cold baptistries or what-you-may-call-'em, after a lifetime adhering to the faith of me fathers, which I've never regretted it," he

said, regretfully; "ah, it's too late for that. For they
doesn't know, nowadays, as to what their own religion
is, fact. There was King Vassily of East Central
Thrace, as kind and honest a fellow as you'd ever want
to know," he went on, wagging his head.

Peregrine, who was, to tell the truth, feeling just
more than a bit restless, caught himself in the act,
mentally issued a rebuke, and looked full of interest.
He was, after all, fond enough of the old man, and he
pitied him with all his heart, for little enough attention
would his palindromes get from Prince Buddy, Prince
Slim, Prince Chuck, his heirs male of the body lawfully
begotten.

"—puts on his full regalia and a proper long face and
off he goes to make his submission and get doused and
take a new name and all the rest o' that clobber, what
was it he was going to be called? Theophilact? Pan-
talemon? Doesn't matter, they says to him. 'Does the
Holy Spirit proceed from the Father *and* the Son or
from the Father *through* the Son?' 'Whichever you
please,' he answers, being of blood royal and a true
gentlemanly pagan with respects for all creeds. Well,
they didn't half do for him, poor fellow, 'heathen' and
'heresiarch' was the mere and mildest of what they
called him as they was a-chopping of him up and
casting the pieces into a whacking great fire before his
very eyes, poor bloke. No, no, me boy, if such is how
they treats you in the name of the Great White Christ, as
some of them calls him, well, give me a great black
one, is all I has to say, arrumph.

"—Now suppose we must get on with it. You has
received your fair entitles and now departs with same,
never returning either alone or with armed host, on
penalty of being flayed alive in order to maintain the
Peace of the Realm, lot of bloody nonsense, and may

the gods—which is to say an allegorical expression of
the infinite attributes of the First Cause—go with you at
your right hand and left, and may you prosper in all
your undertakings, yes, yes, with all my heart, boy,
send us a line when you can, then, and don't wait till
you get settled somewhere, for you're still young and
that may be a long time, for your cullions hasn't cooled
yet; eh?''

And King Paladrine, whose face had grown longer
and longer, embraced his son, who returned the hug
and kiss and said, ''I will, Dadda. Be well, Dadda.
And, oh, say, Dadda, have you heard this one? *'Stop,
murder us not, tonsured rumpots!' ?*''

''What, what?'' exclaimed the king, his face at once
breaking out into an anticipatory grin. ''How does it
go? 'Stop, don't murder—' ''

He had it straight at last, burst into a hearty laugh,
and waved farewell as cheerfully as though he was
seeing Peregrine off to hunt for hares, and back he
went, chuckling and grinning and wagging his head and
repeating the line: a goodly and a doomed old man, and
not until that night when, at wine before his fire he
asked as usual that they ''Send for Perry to give us a
tune and a song,'' was he to remember that there would
never again be at his court a Perry forever.

And precious few tunes and songs.

Thus endeth the first lesson.

* * * *

The roads of Lower Europe, it seemed, were at that
time full of wanderers. Dust lay heavy on the roads at
times, which at other times were churned into mud.
Christians now sat upon the throne of the Caesars,
preaching something called Christian Love, and this

was something of which Peregrine knew not vastly
much; he knew though that now and then the emperors
ceased to preach and slew, with every bit and every
whit as much zeal and bloodshed as though they had
been heathens. And then—then, woe to Christians of
the wrong sect! and, most of all, at all times, no matter
to which sect adhered the current caesar—woe to those
who still and obstinately remained heathen! For
*"Always Rome sends grim gods!"* was their mutter.

However, Peregrine's thoughts were far from grim
right now as he rode off; he was in too many ways glad
to be going. He was riding off, and he was riding well.
Prince Buddy's mother, Queen Calpurnia, second of
his father's lawful wives (Queen Matilda had been
kind to her husband's bastards, but she had been
dead for a few several years), was a good judge of what
was and what was not "best quality second-grade arms
and armor," but she was no judge of mules. And the
stable-thralls, while vowing up and down that this one
was moon-blind and that one was old and the third was
too tough-mouthed to be endured, had all the same seen
to it that Peregrine was furnished as good beasts as were
furnishable. He was of course as sorry as could be to
leave his bluff and well-meaning old father, never to
see him again—as sorry as was possible in a bastard son
who had known since he was three years old that some
day he must do so. And just today the roads were
neither dusty nor muddy, the land was green, the earth
breathed a sweet and not a bitter fragrance, he could not
at all believe that the Empire scene was fully as bad as
his father had hinted at, and, if it were to be so, well, the
Empire was not the whole scene. For the eighteen years
of his young life he had seen nought but the small
Kingdom of Sapodilla. Now he would see more than
that.

He vowed to himself that he would see all that there might be to be seen.

*    *    *    *

The Sovereignty of Sapodilla has—or had— Pannonia on one side and Nararre on the other, being bordered on the north by Lake Illyria and on the south by the Marches of Golconda. Maps are of little use in trying to trace these lineaments, as all the names have been since transferred to other places by right of conquest, by mass migration, and as purely administrative measures as well. When we learn from the pages of Procopius that *Crete* in his time as a Byzantine bureaucrat was held to be officially a part of *Africa*, need nothing surprise us more?

Nothing.

Millet and spelt were growing on both sides of the somewhat narrow and more than somewhat rutted path which was humorously called Highway Number One (wheat being still regarded by the thoroughly backward peasantry of Sapodilla as a new-fangled crop which had yet to prove itself) as Peregrine rode along; and the holes and boulders left by the spring's torrential rains indicated that that same peasantry was up to its favorite outdoor sport of shirking its public duties. He indicated this, with a wave of his slender hand, and a rueful movement of his face, to the one servant allowed him by the customs and counsels of his ancestors— presumably as wise as the day they were uttered.

The servant was, presumably, also as wise as the day he had been uttered, being the slack-mouthed by-blow of the scullery-maid in the lesser-servants' kitchen, commonly called Daft Claudius; Prince Buddy's mother had picked him, too. All questions as to his paternity—which had never been many, the morals of scullery-maids being what they were—had been met with a look of such bafflement on the part of the woman as might have been worthy of a question dealing with the deeper metaphysics. He responded now to his new master's gesture by picking meditatively at a scab in one corner of his mouth, and uttering what was for him a profound and prolonged comment.

"Ah," he said.

Now and then a figure toiling by the barm of the road looked up a moment, resting on a hoe, and gazed at the place in the road which Peregrine and Dafty occupied, and then, blank look unchanged, returned to the task of turning clods. The impression left was that the notion that someone had been going by had been incorrect, and that no-one was going by after all. But Peregrine knew that if he were to turn quickly enough he would just miss meeting with a deeply-interested look. But he did not look back.

At a curve in the road by the side of a hill under a medlar tree two pages in magpie livery slouched to attention. *"PER*-ry!" a voice said, and an unhappy-looking and overfed boy with a medlar in one hand and his penis in the other stood piddling against the tree. He gave the implement a shake or two and let his tunic drop.

"Hey, Buddy. Did you come to see me off? That was nice of you." The pages smirked at each other. They had been selected by the prince's dam for the purpose of introducing him into unnatural vice, as she felt that royal bastardy was bad for the domestic economy.

"Perry, where are you going? Are you going to have adventures? Appledore is up ahead, waiting for you, he wants to get a ride, *she* wouldn't let *him* have a mule, not even a live jackass, the old bitch—"

"Now, Your Royal and Legitimate Highness, let's not talk about your Mommy like that," one of the pages said, primly, casting a quick and languishing look at Peregrine before tossing his head and glancing aside.

"Bugger off, you mothering catamite," said his Royal and Legitimate Highness, aiming a kick at the catamite's crotch. The page clutched, dodged, hissed, and said, venomously, *"Well,* see if I don't tell on *you,* you nasty thing!"

Peregrine reined in. "Appledore is going? Gee, I wonder why—Oh, I guess it's—" and then, seeing the second page regarding him keenly out of the corner of a painted eye, broke in mid-comment. "Goodbye, then, Buddy. Hey, be nice to Dadda, huh?—and I'll send you a souvenir from, uh, somewhere—"

"Send me a clean arsehole for a change," muttered the foul-mouthed prince. His pages squawked their shock at this unseemly insinuation. Buddy, ignoring them, kicked moodily at a fallen medlar, then came up and took hold of his older half-brother's bridle. "Hey, Per, take us with you, I mean, *me,* take us, huh? Per?"

"Gee, Bubber, I can't, you know that. Why, your mom would have the whole Equestrian Order on our trail before you could say, 'Sound the alarm!' "

Prince Buddy scowled, muttered vile things about the entire Equestrian Order and an alleged relationship, damned by men and gods alike, between the Order and its mounts. "Why do the Bastards get ta have alla the fun," he said. *"That's* not fair." But the pages drew nearer and insinuated themselves between the boy and his brother. Prince Buddy began to cry, shook off their hands, struck at them, and then, his corrupted face in his arms, leaned against the tree and wept. The catamite pages gave Peregrine looks half-defiant and half-covetous. He sighed, he winced, blinked, repeated his farewell, and rode on.

About halfway between the medlar tree and the wattle-and-daub hut which marked an important step on his journey, Peregrine saw, leaning on a staff, a figure from whom the bloom of youth had long since departed; sigils and symbols had once been brightly embroidered upon his robe and mantle-cap, but sigils and symbols were bright no longer, robe was rent and spotted in grease, and from one or two holes in the mantle-cap tufts of colorless hair poked out like badly-stooked hay.

"Appledore! You mean, *you* are also one of my father's lovebrats, and they've been keeping it from me? Then where are your mules and—"

The older man grunted and sighed and scratched his aft armpit. "I wish I were . . . chronologically impossible, of course, for all I hear that His Maj was a lusty lad . . . *mule?* Yes, a pair of them, don't you see?" And he lifted first one and then a second spindly shank. Dafty Claud gave a sudden guffaw, as suddenly stopped. "No, no, muh boy. Her Maj, you see, is making a clean, or rather, one might say, a dirty sweep. At one fell swoop she gets rid of you, last of the lot standing between His Maj and her and her own lawful progeny, and *me*. Me! The best royal combination philosopher, metaphysician, sorcerer, and im-promptu-*a capella* bard any weeny court like this is ever likely to see again in *this* cycle of the sun. And appointed her own nephew, that fool, Philander, to take my place. Get the picture?"

A hare hoppited across the road and Appledore, automatically observing its provenance and progress, muttered, "Not unfavorable. —Get the picture?"

Peregrine nodded and sighed. "It's just what I figured, when the kid told me, back there, that you'd be here, and wanting a ride. Gee, poor Dadda!" He thought a moment, added, "Poor Sapodilla, too."

Said Appledore: "Best thing for Sapodilla would be if Buddy broke his neck one night playing steeplechase with those geldings, and Slim caught a sudden dose from the black bottle, disguised as an ague, leaving Chuck. Chuck would soon fix the old lady's wagon."

"Why, Chuck's the worst of the lot!" said Peregrine, dismayed.

The philosopher-sorcerer, and *a cappella* bard nodded. "Exactly. The worst—and the smartest. *He* might just figure out some way to get this so-far-overlooked-but-not-for-long anachronism of a country peacefully into the Empire. In fact, given half a chance, it wouldn't surprise me if Chuck might not wind up as an Imperial Heir of some kind, himself. Co-Sebastocrator, or Conjoint Second Caesar, or something of that sort. Well. Going to stay here all day? With the whole wide world waiting for you? Onward!" He hoisted a grimy sack onto his almost equally grimy shoulder, thumped his staff, and strode on ahead.

Soldiers came out of the wattle-and-daub hut which did duty for frontier-post and customs-house since the former structure had collapsed in last spring's downpour. Usually there were only two men stationed here, but today there were five. They looked apologetic as they gestured to Peregrine to dismount, and sheepish as they made him unload. "You know how it is, huh, Perry," the sergeant said, poking through the equipment. "Doody is doody. Spelled, 'Queen Calpurnia.' " He glanced at a copy of the master-list. "Nope. No contrabands, no, um, contra-indicated articles . . . And what's with you, Doctor Appledore?"

The sage shrugged, dumped his sack empty out onto the road. Soldiers, Peregrine, Daft Claudius, all stared. The sergeant snickered, hastily cleared his throat. Scratched his head. "Bunch a bones. A nold piece a hide. Well. To each his own. Uh, his own taste, I mean. I mean— No export imposts on these articles, Doctor. All respects. Pass, then, in The King's Name. Lots a luck, Perry. Bye, Dafty. Um, uh, your benediction, Doctor?"

Appledore dumped the last bit of bone into the sack and straightened up. He raised his staff. "*Salve adque vale,*" he intoned. "*Nos vobis dominus piscator absit omen.*" He trudged off, dragging the sack.

Peregrine, over the resumed clip-clopping of the mules' hooves, heard one of the soldiers say, low-voiced, half-impressed, half-puzzled, "*Omen,* say, ain't that what the Christians say when they ends their prayers?" If there was an answer, Peregrine didn't hear it. He rode at a brisker pace, pausing only at the brink of the valley which was, in its entirety, part of the Central Roman Empire. Some of it was so far away that its outlines were blurred into a blue-brown mist. A river coiled its way like a lazy snake. A patch of white—that was, must be, a city. An Imperial City! He wished that he had some knowledge of what its name might be. He would have stayed, musing there, had not an odd noise caused him to turn the mule around.

Appledore was arranging the bones as though setting up a class for the study of veterinary anatomy. When he had them outlined he straightened up, gazed at the display with his head cocked, then grunted, spread the tattered and mangy old hide over the lot. "Gift of Queen Calpurnia," he said, "fun-ny sense of humor she's got. Oh, well—." Then he began to intone something which Peregrine recognized as an incantation, in

a tone quite different from the campy tones which
Appledore had used for the ''benediction'' of a short
while back. The sage's voice seemed to come, now,
from deep in his chest, and, now, from high in his nose.
And next he began to beat his staff upon the dirty and
stinking old piece of donkey-hide. The intensity of the
blows increased. Appledore's voice passed into common speech.

''Ass-headed Abraxas, have favor upon the integu-
ments of Thy child!'' he called—and, twice more,
repeated the same set of words. Then, as Perry stared,
fascinated, the hide began a slow rise from the dust of
the road. Appledore threw back his head and brayed
. . . once . . . twice . . . a third time . . . .

No, no. The third bray came not from Appledore at
all. It came from the ass which now stood, a trifle
unsteadily, on the road before them—and now took its
first, uncertain step. And then began to crop the grass
on the barm. Appledore let it feed awhile. Then he took
the belt from around his waist and bound it into a bridle.
Then he gave a skip and a hop and jumped onto the
beast's pin-bones. ''A bit boney,'' he said. ''But 'twill
do. 'Twill do.

''Till better comes our way, that is. *Tchk! Tchk!''*
And, feet splayed out, he set off along the road which
led—Appledore perhaps knew whither. Peregrine did
not. But meant to discover. He pointed his mule's head
after the wizard and was about to dig his heels into the
animal's flanks when he realized that someone was
speaking.

''A useful sort of trick, that,'' said someone. ''It will
be interesting to see if the Child of Abraxas can cross
running water, and how it will behave in the dark of the
moon. It eats grass like a live-born, but, now, I wonder
if it really needs to! It may be mere habit, dimly re-

membered from the days when it was truly alive. Habit is a very peculiar thing, you know.''

Slowly, and with absolute astonishment, Peregrine heard and watched as these comments came from the mouth of his recently-appointed thrall, Daft Claud. ''Very peculiar,'' said Daft Claud, echoing himself, and perhaps echoing some thought of his master's mind. From down the road Appledore's voice drifted back. ''*Yoicks!*'' it was.

''Yoicks!'' repeated Peregrine. Then he said, ''Hey, uh . . . That's the most I ever heard you say before . . . .'' Narrowly he scanned the other's face. It did not seem at all slack-jawed. ''Did the old fellow work a spell on you, too?'' Peregrine asked. Claud shook his head. And, very, very slowly, he grinned. And he winked.

Peregrine said, ''Why, you deceptive son-of-a-bitch! I don't believe you're daft at all! I know you're not!—*Are* you?''

''Nope.''

''Well, then how come that you never let on?—Back there, I mean, at Court?''

''If I had,'' said Claud, ''they'd have made me work twice as hard.''

\* \* \* \*

Lower down, with the afternoon's shadowings lengthening and the sun cooling off, they started up a troop of nummers who had been lying, almost hidden in the grass; and now came flashing up from the thicket like so many quail. They were, or seemed to be, all of a family, large-headed and swart, and they whooped and danced and trotted on their hands, and beat timbrels and cymbals and turned cartwheels and formed pyramids and rolled their eyes beseechingly at him and made such funny grimaces that Peregrine laughed, and tossed them a silver penny. Flashing, it was tossed from hand to hand, till it came between the teeth of the boss-mummer himself, who nipped it and took it out and popped it into his pocket and rolled his eyes and waved his hands and shouted his thanks. Peregrine laughed again, and almost would have stopped, except that Appledore seemed out of hailing distance, so he waved back, and rode on.

Claud rode with him, legs dangling over the baggage. A thrall, by rights, should have been walking; but Peregrine had as much doubts as to Claud's status, these new times, as he had about his own. In Sapodilla, to be sure, Claud had been a thrall. But was he now? In Sapodilla, also, Peregrine had been a royal bastard. Was he still? Bastard? Royal? And what of Appledore? Was he any more what he had been than the bag of bones and dead hide was now what it had been? Life was now being lived in a new place, and, seemingly, according to new rules. Peregrine raised his dark eyebrows and whistled softly to himself.

He was still whistling when they were all suddenly hustled to one side of the road and a troop of strange mules went cantering by, followed by a man on a white horse who did not so much as notice them. And two of the strange mules bore a litter between them, a curtained litter, the horseman caught up with the litter and rode between it and Peregrine's view . . . but not before the curtains had fluttered, the curtains had parted, a face peered out, a pair of eyes met his own, held his eyes—

And then the curtains were drawn as though they had never been undrawn, and in between Peregrine and the curtained litter rode the man on the white horse.

And a very large white horse, and a very large man, they were, too.

"I wonder was she his wife?" Peregrine thought, aloud.

"I wonder was she his wife?" he said to Claud. But Claud was being dumb again, and barely gawped at him and at his question. The cool was thick and deep now, and the road was paved with thick stones, and passed between high hedgerows and orchards and walls. A town lay ahead—one, perhaps, of those white patches which from far, far above had promised Imperial Cities. A man rode a donkey, slouched over, a staff held between arm and side. Peregrine saw that it was Appledore.

"I wonder was she his wife?" he asked him.

" 'Vinegar was the wife of wine,' " the old man muttered. Then his head snapped up. "Ah, Peregrine . . . my thoughts were elsewhere . . . . Was who, you wonder, the wife of whom?"

There was even smoke in the air, first thin, then thick; and the smell of supper. Suddenly the boy's belly awoke, and began to nudge against his ribs. "Didn't you see her, then?" he asked. "The woman in the litter? The man on the white horse? They passed you a while back."

But Appledore insisted that none had passed him. "For," he said, "until I am totally sure of this Child of Abraxas I am riding his dead center down the road, lest he collapse me into a ditch, or such-like. No one could have passed me—unless they passed through me." And he chuckled.

For a moment Peregrine doubted himself. Had he, dreaming, dreamed that, too? Had there indeed been a litter, a curtain, a parted curtain, a glimpse of eyes as deep and bright and lustrous as some forest pool? Had

not, in that moment, her garments moved? Had not a
wisp of something fluttered out upon the air and dust,
trembling and dancing in the sunlight?—and had his
hand clutched after it, dipping and diving in the currents of air?—in that very moment when the alien rider
had come between him and the litter? Had it not?

Had it?

He looked at the hand, clenched upon the reins. And
took the reins in his left hand and slowly, slowly, very
slowly, unclenched the right. Something indeed lay
there, clinging to his sweaty palm, itself all damp and
huddled. He let the leathers drop and guided the mule
with his knees and carefully plucked the thing up with
his fingers. It was a feather, he did not know what kind
of a feather. And still clinging to it, as he raised it nearer
to his eyes, was a sort of faint fragrance. A sort of
scented musk. A hint of gardens richer than any which
grew in the thin soil of his neglected native land.

A hint of the flesh of women, and this, too, richer
than any known to him before.

Very carefully he felt for his pouch, and very carefully he took out the bit of parchment in which his old
nurse-nanny had wrapped him up a golden luck-penny.
And very carefully he placed the one upon the other.
And very carefully rewrapped and returned the small
packet and drew tight the thongs of the pouch. A
moment he thought, and now he knew he dreamed.
And then he took the reins and whooped and shouted.
"Appledore! Claud! Mules! Child of Abraxas! Are you
not all as hungry as I?"

\* \* \* \*

Any dreams which he may have dreamed about
gourmandizing amidst the presumably rich cuisine of

the Central Roman Empire vanished like a pricked bubble at the inn. "Landlord!" he shouted, joyfully, having handed over the mules and the Child of Abraxas to a wall-eyed hostler with a prominent goitre: "Landlord! What can you give us for our supper?" And he flung himself onto a bench. Moving slightly, a second later, and gazing upwards, a trifle bemusedly, in search of the fowl which must, not very many minutes ago, have perched on the very beam above that very bench. From this search he was recalled by the landlord's voice.

"What can *I* give you?" the voice asked. There was a silence. The time might have been better spent, the voice and even more the silence hinted, in considering . . . perhaps Longinus, *On The Sublime*. "For *your* supper?"

The silence fell again.

"Beans," the voice said.

The first silences had really been the landlord's silences. This one was definitely Peregrine's. It was not a meditative, it was an incredulous silence. He had been expecting to hear mention of, as it might be, breaded kid's kidneys. Or quails in aspic. Or a suckling pig, with truffles in its nose. *"Beans?"* he demanded.

Something in his tone there must have been which disturbed the landlord. There was a shuffling noise, as he came closer into the dim light shed by the fire; a thin man with protruding eyes and a pendulous belly. He stopped, the shuffling sound did not. Behind him came she who could only have been the landlord's wife; that is to say, the landlady. A fat woman, with sunken eyes and a pendulous bosom.

"Is there something the matter with beans?" he asked.

"Something you don't like?" she enquired.

"You some kind of a Pythagorean, or something, you don't care for beans?"

There was a mutter from the other side of the fireplace. "Them Pythagoreans," another voice said. "Always advertising, and that's why they got all the money."

"What about all the starving children in Erythrea?" the landlady demanded, truculently. "You think that they wouldn't be *glad* to have some beans?"

"They'd *love* to have some beans," the landlord said.

Peregrine considered matters. Perhaps he had been too hasty. This was, after all, not Sapodilla. There, beans had been thrall-food. Did the small Peregrine misbehave? "Think you're much, don't you, just because you're the king's bastard? Go and eat beans with the thralls." —But that was there. And then, who knew what sort of a lavish way they had of preparing beans, here in the Central Roman Empire?

"I, too, would love to have some beans," he said, after an instant. Landlord and landlady beamed at him, transfigured. They lifted their hands and, slowly, hieratically, they made that gesture of which he had often heard.

"In the Name of the Father, and of the Mother, and of the Holy Son," they said, more or less in unison. "We bid you thrice welcome." And busied themselves with cauldron, ladle, and with pots.

Peregrine felt an elbow in his ribs. Appledore whispered, "I was looking forward to something like this," his voice filled with relish " 'The *Mother*'! I was hoping there'd be some new heresies, I used to get so tired of the old ones! Oh boy!"

And on Peregrine's other side, Claud leaned over heavily and said, "Syncretistic influences of Isis-worship, how much you want to bet?"

Appledore, forgetting to whisper, said, "Do you really think so? You know, I shouldn't be a bit surprised!"

The mutter from the other side of the fireplace became visible, and the floor shook beneath the tread of one of the largest (and ugliest) men whom Peregrine had ever seen. His eyes were large and bloodshot and he had in each nostril a larger beard than Peregrine had in either armpit, and his lubber-lips sagged, disclosing large and cracked and yellowy-greenery teeth, rather like those of a quarrelsome horse. "Say. Strangers." he said. "Just what religion do you belong to. Hey?"

Peregrine held his breath. Appeldore promptly answered, "The True One."

"And which one is that. Hey?" demanded the Anti-Pythagorean.

Resolutely, Appledore said, "There is only one." More than resolutely. Almost reprovingly. The ugly one swayed on his vast, splayed feet a moment, still muttering. Then he retreated. But still muttering. The landlady looked up from the cauldron to ask her husband something. He, in turn, looked over to the new guests.

"Will you have bread, then?" he asked.

They nodded. And then Appledore was moved to say, "It is, after all, the basic substance of the Holy Sacrament—" He was warned by the visible change in his hosts' faces to stop. And asked—perhaps unwisely—though by that time it perhaps scarcely mattered—"It *isn't*? Then, for pity's sake, what *is?*"

The landlord was decent enough to answer the question, before picking up an axe and dodging around the fireplace to attack them. "*Beans!*" he shouted.

"Heretics!" shrilled his wife, flailing her ladle and tucking up her skirts. "Donatists! Mandeans! Gnostics! Orthodox! Monophysites!" She came leaping and waving the huge ladle like a battle-mace. And the floor trembled again as the ugly giant came thundering forward, but this time stopping stock-still in the face of the landlady's vituperation.

"Yer wrong on them charges," he said. "They're Pythagoreans, I tell ya! I can smell 'em! I can tell 'um in the dark—"

"Let me at them! Let me by! I'll skewer their heretical tripes!" the landlord shouted. "The— the—the *Nestoreans!*"

He dodged to one side around the ugly giant, only to come smack against his wife, skittering around the other. The pot tipped into the fire, filling the air with steam and sharp shouts of pain and dismay, and all the while the ugly giant, meanwhile kicking aside the benches, asked, rhetorically, "Who was the original beans-hater? Answer me that? Pythagoras! Wasn't it? Wasn't it? I want a Yes or No from ya—where are they? I'll killum, I'll killum!—It was Pythagoras. Wasn't it?"

Later, in the darkness, Peregrine said, panting, "Well, you wanted to hear of new heresies. I hope you found this one new enough for your taste." Fortunately the hostler had been very slow, and had not as yet unbridled the mules. They had lost part of the baggage, but they still had their hides. And so, judging by his protesting bray, so had the Child of Abraxas.

Claud, breathing thoughtfully, asked, "Appledore, was it Pythagoras who was the original beans-hater?"

Appledore's reply was succinct. "Yes," he said.

Claud let out another thoughtful breath. "Well," he said, after a moment, "maybe he knew what he was doing. . . ."

\* \* \* \*

By the light of the half-moon they paused to consider a moment at the crossroads the other side of the town. Appledore pointed to a small shrine. "Some pagan image stood in yon niche," he said. "Some tangible reminder of the ancient and intangible faith of our forefathers. Personally, I was raised at my mother's knee as a Neoplatonist, but—"

"Your mother's son's head may rest in yon niche," said Peregrine, impatiently, "if we don't decide which way we're going to move on—and decide the right way—"

Appledore gestured him to silence and patience. The philosopher divided his beard with both hands and stroked each clump. "To the right," he said, musingly, after a moment, "the road leads *down,* down into the great heartland, so to speak, of the Central Roman Empire, where there is to be sure both repressive government and repressive religious orthodoxy, with each heresy striving to become orthodoxy—but at least the orthodoxy and the heresy is of a more familiar and predictable kind. To the middle," he gestured, "the road leads on more or less, seemingly, on this same level . . . perhaps because this same level is neither up nor down but as it were—"

"*Appledore!*"

"—that one finds such unexpected oddities as that Bean Cult back there, interesting concept, perhaps their god speaks to them from their bellies?—well, well, and so," he went on, hastily, "onward!"

But his dilatory acquiescence was not sufficient to restore Peregrine to the mood of high hopes and pleasant anticipation with which he had commenced his journey. Was it worthy, indeed, of being called a journey when it had not even an approximate destination, no set goal? . . . Was it to be nothing more than successive and dangerous encounters with fanatics and with madmen, from one of which he would, eventually, not emerge? The night itself was not blacker than his mood, which last was at that moment not even illuminated by so much as a half-hope as the former was by a half-moon.

Chilled and grim, he tugged his cloak out from a saddlebag, and, having indifferently pulled it more-or-less around his shoulders and sides, sat huddled disconsolate upon his mule, scarcely caring which way it was carrying him, as not knowing for what purpose, and to what end. His heart, usually light enough, lay heavily within his breast.

From this mood he was, if not exactly aroused, at any rate diverted by the sudden awareness that his two companions had halted. He had opened his mouth in order to express, not so much his precise puzzlement at that moment as his general vexation in that hour, when Claud, with a gentleness that Peregrine (thinking over the gesture afterwards, and again) ceased not to marvel at, moved swiftly and laid his roughened hand across the other young man's mouth. Sheer astonishment kept Peregrine quiet, resentment—''For all that we are both bastards, I am the bastard of a king by a yeoman-farmer's daughter, and he the bastard of a kitchen-wench by no-one-knows-what-sire: How doth he dare to lay his hand upon my lips? a gesture suitable only to and among the closest intimates''—mingling with astonishment—''And where and from whom did he learn to move so gently?''—caution, not yet alarm—''What portends this singular and sudden deed?'' So Peregrine made no sound, and automatically his hands and his knees brought the mule to halt.

The trees to left and right were but black masses against the night sky; but ahead, ahead, between them and the half-moon, the trees were grey and ghosty and seemed to catch the obscured and occluded moonlight, and suck it in, transmute and transform it, and shine with the now changed element, releasing it as a new radiance, their borders glowing and trembling with the nimbus of the nocturnal aurora.

And beyond all this, moonlit meadow seemingly riding on a cloud of dew, half-way between dew-dampened sod, sodden with dew, and the descending dew and the tree-tops, in the false light and false perspective, lights were seen which were neither moon nor stars; voices were heard which were not voices of which he had any familiarity; they muttered, they croaked, and now and again they rose and soared in a chant which was betimes both frightening and beautiful.

Peregrine was not aware of having moved. Indeed, was not the purpose of the halt, of his cojourner's gesture, that they move not, lest they move into danger? Or—? Nor could he credit that the scene, whate'er it was, in the black, black meadow, moved itself towards them . . . Something was ruling in that night which made its own motions and its own immobility and ruled and reigned by its own laws. Something was of lightly moving in that glimmer and that glow which may have been man and which may have been beast or which may have been god or gods. He was suddenly certain of being in the near but very presence of a great mystery, and he was still (save unless he did in sooth move) and he awaited. He heard the measured croaking of a hundred frogs, he heard the bellow, muted, muted, of a multitude of bulls, he heard the belling of a hundred sounds as in one chorus, he heard another noise and another song and chant, and either from near and low, or from far and so muted and mellowed, the words, the words, *"The Goat . . . The Goat . . . The Great . . . The Great . . . The Black . . . The Black . . . The Great Black Goat . . .*

*"The Great Black Goat . . ."*

The words died away, the words echoed, the words sang to each other in his inner ear, his flesh moved, the words changed, the old words echoed from some distant choir, antiphonally, new words, new chant, a climax reached, or being reached . . .

*"Take . . ."*

"Take . . ."

*"Take . . ."*

"Red . . ."

*"Red . . ."*

*"Bread . . ."*

"Bred? . . ."

*"Bread . . ."*

"The knife . . ."

*"The knife . . ."*

". . . cut . . ."

*"Cut . . ."*

"Red . . ."

*"Red . . ."*

Peregrine felt the mystery quicken and increase its hold upon him, and fear grew within him, that he should hear, who was no postulant, no initiate, should hear this great mystery, this massive mystery, he knew not for sure which it was, of, perhaps? Dionysus? of mayhap, Hercules Manslayer? With one part of him he desired only to allow nothing to stop which would move him closer, and with another part he feared to do other than to withstand this other; the chant and song and drone continued, it halted, it went on, it stopped, it would never stop, it continued, rose and fell, rose and rose, high, higher, highest, it reached into a scream, it wailed away into a groan, it was as sweet as honey and

as hot as love, his muscles moved, his head swam, he
was falling, he was falling, it was illusion, delusion, he
would fall only if he did not yield, such power of his
own could he wield that he need not . . . .

Hooves beat upon the soil of night, they were moving, they had moved on, there were many of them,
there was the man on the white horse, *there* was the
litter, where were Peregrine's companions, for now he
could point them out to them, the beasts which bore the
litter and the rider upon the great white horse. Of his
companions he could see nought. He rode close to the
litter, he would not presume to place his hands upon the
curtain, yet he presumed to raise his eyes not boldly but
quite calmly to her guardian and to say to him, "Sir, I
am Peregrine by name and by my present motion; I am
son to a king, but never heir to him in any degree known
to law. Know that never could I, would I, intend or
furnish harm to this lady therein, whom you guard and
whom, I must suppose, you guide. May I at least know
more?"

The large man upon the large horse said, civilly,
quietly, "In this age of change and of decay, of progress and retrogression, many are those who must move
on if they at least would stand still."

"Stand still? No, sir, I would see unknown islands
arising fresh from the sea at dawn. I would see the
lamps of new cities riding like ships' lights in the
darkness soon to give way to morning. I would look
upon the walls of great cities and I would see their gates
swing open to me and I would enter, sir, I would enter
and see new things. I—"

And the man said, "You would know more. You
would know that this lady whom I guard and whom I
guide is called Princess Poppyseed? Know it, then.
You would see gates swing open? Know, then, this as
well: *There is no escape, save through the Gates which*

*our fathers would have died rather than enter, prefer-*
*ring death in its familiar forms to life, therein, in its*
*unfamiliar . . . ."*

The curtains of the litter parted, the face of the young
woman was revealed, she looked upon him with her
shining eyes, he felt that his bastardy meant nothing to
her, that it meant less than nothing to her. Her eyes
glowed like lamps, and in the darkness of that night he
felt the illumination of strange light. He saw his hand
moving, saw it moving towards the embroidered curtains of the gorgeous seat on which she rode. He saw
dawn breaking, and he saw Claud riding stolidly beside
him, and Appledore ahead, wearing a look weary and
spent, yet withal prepared, withal by no means devoid
of strength. He looked for the rider on the white horse,
and he saw him no more than he saw the Rider's ward.
A sound rose in his throat and broke upon his lips, and
no hand moved now at all to keep his silence.

Appledore stirred, said, low, "Of what we have seen
and heard, we three, this night which has now ended, it
would be best, I think, if we are never called upon to
speak of between us ever again."

But Peregrine knew that he himself had seen more
than either of the other two. And he kept his hopes. And
he kept his silence.

And the greyness of the earliest morning turned a soft
and a warm color, and the Sun came swimming up from
wherever the Sun had spent the night. And the birds
took their small heads from under their small, warm
wings, and all the birds began to greet the day. And
Peregrine knew that, whatever the day should bring, or
the night succeeding this day, whatever danger night
succeeding night should or would or might succes-
sively bring, Peregrine knew that he was able to meet it.
And to endure it.

# PART
# 2

Part of Peregrine's mind continued to be occupied with the remembrance of the eyes of Princess Poppyseed; part of it returned again and again to the word of the Rider on the White Horse. *"There is no escape, save through the Gates which our fathers would have died rather than enter, preferring death in its familiar forms to life, therein, in its unfamiliar . . . ."* And it was with a mixture of lust, love and foreboding, that he attended to his gear, testing swordblade and arrowhead with his thumb, and seeing to the replacement of the missing foodstuffs and examining the hooves and shoes of the mules.

In these essential tasks his moody attentiveness was almost matched by Claud's moody inattentiveness. In the short time since their having left Sapodilla the page's slack mouth had become firm, his dull eyes had begun to show an unfamiliar sparkle, and the sores round his face had quite dried up. Even now, although he was subdued, his manner was new and different. And so, almost the moment he turned abruptly to speak, Peregrine had expected him to do so.

Said Claud: "I need a lay."

Said Perry: "You won't get it from me."

"Say, I ain't your half-brother, and I know you ain't either. No, I thought that the girls here were the same as the girls back home, only, like I heard they know a thing or two as the home-girls don't. Well, this one in the kitchen here, so her name's Amoeba, or something like that, nice pair of—Well, I says, 'Girl, I got something real big for you and there's nobody in the stable now, let's go, hey?' And—you know what she says to me? You're not a-going to believe this maybe, but I swear by my cod it's true: She says, *'What will you pay me?'* "

"Oh!" said Peregrine, intrigued, "I've heard about that. 'Whores,' they call them, don't they? Well, go on—"

"Is that what it means? I thought it was just a word. Well, the long and short of it is, she says it's a *sin*. And what does *that* mean? She says, 'If I got to risk hell-fire, you got to pay me for it, Big Something,' she says. Then she started lecturing me about my immortal soul, and, before long, you know, it wasn't big at all, anymore. And I says, 'Forget it,' and went to muck out the mules' stalls. I mean, it's not as though she was a priestess at some great temple where the girls 'hang up their girdles for the goddess,' as they say: she's just a *girl!*—Funny kind of religion, is what I call it. Asceticism is one thing, an interesting philosophical discipline; but I ain't no philosopher, I'm only a healthy young fellow with a heavy prong: *cacadaemon!*"

And he spat into the straw.

Appledore, who had been listening with only now and then a glint of wry amusement, now said, gravely, "Bring me the skin and the bones of Cleopatra the Queen, and I will enconjur her up into full life for you and your pleasure, Stripling."

"I wouldn't consider it," said Claud, after considering it a moment. "She might leave splinters."

Peregrine began to heave harness up onto the beasts. "Enough of this bawds' prattle," he said, concealing his grin. "Onward!"

They took a back-path, grass-grown, in preference to the main roads, for rumor had it that no less than three successive cities through which the highways passed had proclaimed their own Caesars Augustus and were prepared to march on Ravenna and depose whatever claimant was currently (and precariously) occupying the Imperial Throne: but nobody in town knew which city had proclaimed what Caesar. Even assuming that the three travellers were able to find out in sufficient advance to declare for, say, Marcus, instead of for, say, Romulus or Valentinus—or what might ever be the names—they were still certain, at best, to lose their beasts and gear to the commissary-major.

Caesar might have one name, or he might have a different name, but Caesar always had a commissary-major. So Appledore said.

"I was once proclaimed Caesar myself," he said, as they wound upwards between boulders and scree along a trail no wheel had rolled, surely, over.

"And I was once proclaimed Son of the God at the Temple of the Oasis of Jupiter-Ammon-Alexander."

"No, for true, Perry. It was in Byzantium, where anything can happen. Troops of soldiers were rioting for their back pay and had looted the wine shops. *'Proclaimed is Chrysodorus, chaste champion of orthodoxy!'* one band was shouting. And, across the square, another outfit was shouting, *'Chrysodorus is a crypto-Monophysite, and buggers little boys! Proclaimed is Basilianus, conqueror of the Avars!'* —or whichever barbarian nation had made a temporary submission most recently, for ready cash and a chance to send back for fresh horses. Well, gentlemen, they had somehow gotten a purple robe and were tussling over it and someone tugged at the moment when someone else had stopped tugging, and it went sailing through the air and by the inscrutable ordinance of the Fates, lo! it fell right smack onto *me!* Sudden silence in the square. And one soldier—a Norsky, a Varangian, by the looks of him—yelled, '*A sign! A sign from the Great White Christ!*' They always talk that way, you know.

"Next thing I knew, they had hoisted me onto a shield, after asking in the most deferential manner conceivable in a bunch of thugs who had gotten half-soused and could as easily have subjected me to the most conceivable tortures, 'What's your name, O Brother? And how will your Imperial Highness choose to be known?' 'Julius the Second,' I said. And they went staggering through the precincts of the Golden Mile, bellowing, '*Proclaimed is Julius II, chaste champion of orthodoxy, conqueror of the Avars, Caesar Augustus most serene, Sebastocrator, Pantocrator, Autarch, Autocrat, and unquestionable Emperor of the East!*' "

Peregrine ducked to avoid a low-crouching branch. "Zeuspater!" he muttered.

"They went looking for a crown, and scarlet, pearl-encrusted slippers and all the rest of the Regalia, but on the way they found another drammery they hadn't cracked; when they were totally in liquor, Your Servant to Command slipped out of the purple robe and draped it around the big Norsky; then I skedaddled for The Sweet Waters of Asia and parts more distant as fast as my legs, the ferry-wherry, a relay of swift horses and my by-no-means-boundless purse would take me. For as a philosopher, I wanted no part of the precarious Purple."

"*Chronos!*" whispered Claud. The mules strained at the boulders and slipped on the scree. The air was getting thinner, and was scented with pine-balsam. "Did you ever hear what happened afterwards?"

Appledore nodded, then set his wizard's cap to rights again.

"It seems that when they sobered up and saw the big Varanguard wearing the purple robe which none of them, including himself, could remember having put there, '*A sign from The Great White Christ!*' they cried, and they proclaimed *him* Caesar under the style and title of Isidore III—"

"So *that* was Isidore III! I've heard of *him!*"

Appledore smiled, thinly. "No doubt you have. He not only failed to pay the promised donatives, but was found one night wandering around Hagia Sophia with a torch in one hand, a spike in the other, gouging out the right eye from the mosaics of the Great White Christ, on the grounds that that one had taken over *all* the attributes of Odin the Wise, who had sacrificed the eye in return for wisdom. He was promptly proclaimed a heretic, and burnt alive in the Hippodrome between the third and fourth races being held in honor of the Feast of the Virgin Birth. Later on, however, I heard that he had been canonized by the Isaurians as a proto-iconoclast, under the style and title of Saint Isidore the Insane. Heigh-ho."

"You were well out of it."

"I was *very* well out of it. The pickings may have been thin, back in the Sovereignty of Sapodilla (last pagan kingdom in Lower Europe), but life was a lot safer. Until there came Queen Calpurnia, the sunderer of delights, the blighter of tenure in office, and the lawfully-wedded mother of Prince Buddy, Prince Slim, and Prince Chuck."

"Heigh-ho," said Peregrine.

"Heigh-ho," said Appledore once again.

"Heigh-ho," said Claud, coming out of a revery.

"What is that up ahead?" asked Claud, after a moment. "Mist?"

"The weather and the time of day are not right for

mist," Sage Appledore said, consideringly. "I should estimate that the chances are one in two that 'tis the smoke of a medium-sized campfire, and one in two that 'tis the breath of a rather small dragon. Let me see," he muttered, as he puttered in his geezlesack, "do I, amongst my geezles, include a leaf or so of—"

He was still muttering and puttering when they found themselves ascending onto a plateau, one side of which was faced with the gaunt escarpment of a rocky cleft, in the side of which was a cave. And in front of the cave, breathing lazily into the thin grey air, and looking rather as though it were observing the general effect with interest, lolled a rather small dragon, in size no larger than a common cart-horse. Peregrine reached for his sword, at once realized that such a weapon was of little use against a dragon, upon whom (it is a commonplace, known to every child) there are only three places wherein a fatal wound can be inflicted, and those only by thrusting deeply; reached for his spear, realized that the spears were with Claud, tried simultaneously to turn and beckon to his man and to keep his mule from twisting its head out of its halter and get a better look at what was crouching there—

"—of dragonbane?" muttered Appledore. And forthwith, "*Ah!*" he uttered, and held it up for all to see. The wind shifted, the mules screamed and reared up, all three, the Child of Abraxas issued the first half of a terrified bray, and the dragon unfolded its wings with a sound like trees whipping in a high wind, sent forth a hiss which caused the dust and rubble for ten feet before it to rise, and, with every appearance of terror and dismay, flew more-or-less straight up into the air, its feet churning frantically as though for purchase, and soared off into the distance.

The animals subsided as though more than somewhat

ashamed, and, indeed, the ass, instead of issuing the
other half of its bray, gave a rather sheepish-sounding
cough instead, and pretended to crop a mouthful of
non-existent grass. Claud leaped off his mule. "Ho, a
dragon, a treasure, a hoard!" he cried, scurrying into
the cave. "Ibs!"

"Dibs!" said Appledore, after he had collected his
senses. "Stop, you selfish oaf, stop! It was *my* geezle,
*my* dragonbane!" and he slid to the ground and followed after the lad. Peregrine gazed after the rapidly-
dwindling speck in the sky, and, somewhat slowly,
followed them into the cave.

But the creature had evidently been extremely new to
the treasure-trove business, for all that they found in the
cave in the way of a hoard were three oboli and a
drachma, all of a very devaluated coinage; and one very
battered bracelet inscribed *Cailus loves Mariamne* and
made of base metal.

"So much for your ibs and your dibs," Peregrine
said, disgustedly. And added, with a lofty note, "I
hope this will be a lesson to you henceforth," and
turned to leave, disdainfully, the effect being rather
spoiled by his at once tripping and falling almost on his
face. He cursed, and tried at the same time to nurse his
stinging toe and aching wrist, gave over both attempts,
and turned and scuffled angrily in the dust of the cave
floor. A rather rusty iron ring had done the mischief,
and he gave it an annoyed wrench. Up it flew, and
attached to it was a carrying-case of moldering leather.

"What is this, what is this?" he asked, half-
aloud—and, seeing his companions looking from him
to it with faces surprised and expectant and abashed, he
added (feeling he could, under the circumstances, do
no less and no other): "Share and share alike . . ."
They bowed their heads—to raise them at once.

"Pray, open it at once, dear princely Peregrine,"
urged Appledore, in an all but fawning voice. "For
although an archaic code may inhibit my saying *Prince*
Peregrine, still and nonetheless your generosity is no
less than princely. Ope, ope, ope," he gestured.

And Claud, swallowing noisily, and gazing at the
dusty case with glistening eyes said, "Teach us a lesson, sweet master, by leaving us see just what it is
which you're so kindly going to share, huh?"

The case was locked with a small bronze clasp of
cunning craftsmanship, depicting two copulating serpents with tiny eyes of a rufous stone. Between the
three of them, however, they had not so much as a
nutpick, and Peregrine was loath to spoil the item by
forcing it. He unsheathed his sword and thrust it into the
crumbling leather as easily as though it had been the
cloth around a ripened cheese; and there fell out,
though not before he could catch it, a diadem set all
around with enamels and with polished gems. For a
moment they stood there, dumbstruck, Peregrine with
the diadem in his hands, and Claud and Appledore with
theirs outstretched still. Then he walked out into the
daylight, and they hastened after him.

Appledore bent over to examine it, and then, either
from awe or from a desire to examine it more closely,
he knelt. After a moment, Claud did the same. Said the
sage, "This is surely the very coronet of Queen
Cleopatra. Unless," he said, "it may on the other hand
assuredly be the royal head-ring of the King of the
Ephts—yes! yes!—that is—ah, no! no! 'Tis the very
crown worn by the Ptolemies of Upper Southeast Cy-
prus! Or . . . uh . . ." and he fell silent, observing
the curious designs and the sparkling stones.

"What it is," Claud said, "it is a *crown*, that is what
it is. My dear master, you are surely meant to be a king,

being of blood royal, and the Fates had a better share in store for you than piddly bitty Sapodilla, huh?''

"Huh?" said Peregrine, squinting at them, at it, at the now empty sky, and back to *it* again, said, "I don't want to be a king. I want to travel around lightly and encounter adventures and have a lot of interesting fun. What's the point of being a bastard if people are going to try to make you a king? Look at my poor dadda, King Paladrine, and his nasty old queen, him worrying where next year's taxes are going to come from with the peasants always saying, 'Crops poor, why you no make rain, King?' and her always nudging him for new liveries for her new servants—look at all those half-an-obolus Caesars Augustus always wondering if a guards' regiment is going to disembowel them because some new pretender has promised a bigger donative or a half-mad patriarch will stir up the populace on a charge of indulging the heretics—

"No, friends, No *sir!* I don't want to be a king!"

There was a silence there on the plateau. Then Claud gave a disappointed grunt, and Appledore a weary sigh. Then the latter said, "Well, well, and I thought perhaps to end my days as the patronee of a powerful king, and teaching philosophy in a stoa, but it seems that no one nowadays is minding the stoa. So be it, boy. Shall we then return the crown to its previous concealing dust, and let the dragonlet return to add to its hoard? It might serve as bait as it were, and you—for I shall long have gone to learn true philosophy from the spirit lips of Aristotle and Epictetus in the mead of golden as-phodel—but you might mark its location in your mind, and return hither some day to recruit your fortune from the recruited hoard, eh?" There was a longer silence, Peregrine plucked at his red lips.

"No . . ." he said. "No . . . Let us wrap it in a

napkin and conceal it in our baggage, say, between the pod of musk and the ten measures of barley meal. Perhaps . . . That is, who knows . . . I mean . . .

"See to that, Claud," he concluded, as though a bit annoyed that no one else had suggested anything, either, concerning the purpose and future of carrying the mysterious crown with them. And his fingers stroked the new soft beard slowly springing up on his cheeks and chin, then he mounted his mule and rode slowly off, they presently following him after the new-found treasure had been stowed away.

*    *    *    *

Their next encounter was at a narrow cottage beside a grove standing in a dale, where a woman standing in a door about to empty a basin of dishwater gave a startled shriek and disappeared inside. "Ee! Reverend Mother! Men!" they heard her shrill. And in another moment out came bustling a stout and redfaced woman in a white robe and a black wimple, who sank, staff in hand, onto her knees before Appledore; who gazed at her with the almost utmost astonishment.

"O handsome, stalwart and lusty sir," she cried, "spare, O spare the chastity of these religious ladies—meself included, for all that I'm long in the tooth, sure, isn't me dedicated chastity as dear to me as to me younger sisters?—who have been just after fleeing from Rome, Boadicea is me name, and I come of a good, a fine, and why should I conceal the fact from yezz?—a royal family, in me native Celtland —fleeing from Rome where the accursed Stilicho, the Sassenach dog—for is there but the spit out of a devil's mouth the difference between a Goth and a Saxon?—has been after extinguishin' the sacred fire upon the altar of our Lady Vesta, may he niver know a moment's rist, may his wife rigularly cuckold him with Athiopians, and may his yard niver grow hard again as long as he lives, which may it be short! Sweet honey and noble harseman, say that yezz'll spare our maidenheads, and may Our Howly Mither Vesta peep down upon yezz favorably from Hivven: do, sir! Do!''

Appledore twirled his withered moustachios, and gave a languishing leer, which he made haste to extinguish. ''Hem! and, Harrumph, Reverend Madame, have no uncertainty but that my natural and inevitable lusts, though certainly awakened at the sight of your comely form and figure, will instantly subside upon learning your identity. However, weakened by years and by many fasts as I am, can I vouch for the constancy of my companions in this matter?''

The Chief Vestal Virgin let her jaw to drop at the sight of Peregrine and Claudius, who at that moment came cantering into sight, ''Oh sure and be Vesta!'' she exclaimed, ''but ain't there a two more o'thim, and two more of us a-trimblin' with fear in the' cottage there, it bein' all the bit o' convent that we've got to oursilves these days, which makes one a-piece for the Christian divvils to try to ravish: Och, allana! me deary sisters! After being the coddled daughters of hathen Rome, to be humped in a hovel by a trio of tramps!'' And she lifted up her voice in a Brythonic, or, as it may have been, a Goidelic lamentation, in which she was interrupted by a third female.

''Your keening smacks a trifle of impiety,'' said she, ''Reverend Mother. Now that the Sacred Fire, attended with the infinite diligence of antiquity and splendor, has been suppressed, is it perhaps not inevitable that our vows of chastity be suppressed with it? If the inscrutable decrees of The Fates decree that we be ravished in this wretched retreat, why, what can we do, save submit seriously to Their sacred though severe decree?''

Mother Boadicea glared at her, venomously. ''Shut yer gob, ye whure!'' she said; ''or I'll give yezz such a puck wid me staff—''

By this time the third Vestal Virgin had emerged once again from the cottage, though she seemed uncertain upon which side of this knotty piece of theology to range herself; and both Peregrine and Claud reined in their beasts and all three faced all three. Truth to tell, the former could not recollect if the Virgins of the Vestal Fire had been professed at the age of seven or seventeen, or whether they had been supposed to serve until thirty-six or sixty-three; and he was fairly certain that he had heard of the extinguishing of the Fire by General Stilicho some several years back—an act which had resounded like a thunderclap throughout what remained of pagan Europe; in short, though the Mother Superior of what remained of the Vestal Virgins was indeed as she herself had acknowledged, viz. ''long in the tooth,'' the other two seemed by no means young—certainly, not as either he or Claud were prepared to understand Youth.

''Neither force nor constraint shall touch a thread of your garments, Reverend Lady,'' he said, straight-faced; ''nor those of your fellow-religious. For we have all three of us been raised by good pious pagan mothers,'' and the long and short of it all was that before another few minutes had passed, the three vestals, still as virgin as before, were preparing dinner for Peregrine, Appledore, and Claud, out of the travellers' provisions.

''Would that Stilicho had never extinguished the Sacred Fire,'' observed Peregrine, wiping his mouth.

The Vestal Virgins echoed his regret, though not all, perhaps, with the self-same heartiness; ''—or,'' he went on, ''burned the Sibylline Books—''

At this reference to the other notorious act of the great Gothic general (who seemed, great or not, one way or the other to be obsessed with fires), the Mother Superior, who had needed no third invitation to address herself to the mugs filled from the wine skin, winked and smiled.

''Eh?'' said Peregrine.

Mother Boadicea repeated the grimace, this time laying an index finger alongside of her nose.

''Why, whatever do you mean?'' Peregrine enquired. ''Did he not burn the Sibylline Books?''

At this Mother Boadicea raised her eyebrows, pursed her lips, smoothed her skirts, and looked elaborately half-way over her left shoulder and, in short, appeared so much the very picture of a woman who wishes it known that she knows something which others know not: ''Whisht!'' she said. ''Coosha, coosha, He did, did he?—may no good cess befall his seed—ah, well, if you know that for a fact, far be it from me to tell yezz itherwise. Curiosity killed the cat, and, says I, serve it right for letting 'I dare not' wait upon 'I will.' And if yezz was ivver to hear that some pious soul, the while the rest of them were runnin' around wringin' their hands and wailin' like the beansidh, tuk and wrapped the Howly Volumes up in her pettycuts, substithuthin thereunfor an unexpurgated edition of the Satyricon in five volumes, which the cursed man nivver nowticed, nor could, bein' unable to read a word not in his native Gothic—why, me pretty squireen, I give ye lave to deny the intire story: So there.'' And with that she gave her coiffed and wimpled head an emphatic nod, and downed the rest of the goblet.

Peregrine pondered on these cryptic words, absent-mindedly refilling the cup, taking the merest sip from it, and replacing it on the rustic table within reach of the lady's hand, and then staring as it might have been through an invisible hole in the hovel wall some several inches above her head: and she watched him with a mixture of shrewdness and satisfaction, now and then delicately wiping her mouth upon her habit—for (as she had often reminded him) she had been reared and bred with the utmost delicacy in her native Celtland, where the art of delicate breeding was understood, appreciated, and exercised as nowhere else.

At length the lad gave a deep sigh, and said aloud, though clearly to himself, "Ah well, although one cannot escape one's fate, much would one wish to love to get a line on what that fate might be, particularly if one is the youngest bastard son of the last pagan king in Lower Europe, Paladrine of Sapodilla; and hence cast upon the world with little enough, of course, if it enables one to rescue from the grossest barbarity a delicately reared daughter of the kings of Celtland; heigh ho!"

Reverend Mother Boadicea's expression softened somewhat during this address, and she gave a sound not unlike a hiccough—to name no less refined form of eructation. "And what would yezz be givin' to obtain that oracle?"

"I would give," said Peregrine, in a faraway tone, "I would give the Crown of the Kings of the Ephts—"

The Chief Vestal Virgin gave a great start. "Ah, and the very mention of its name constitutes a Word of Great Power!" she whispered. "Ye don't mean to be sayin' that ye have the—" and her voice died away and she looked at him in the dimlight with widened and reddened eyes.

"If you'll show me yours," said Peregrine softly,
"I'll show you mine—"

\* \* \* \*

"Hey, master," said Claud, shoving him rather
roughly. Nearby, a mule snored softly . . . softly, that
is, for a mule.

"Whuzz?" inquired Peregrine. Through the chinks
in the leanto he could see the deliquescent stars.

"Were you having a nightmare?"

"Whurmph . . ."

"You kept saying, *'Burn the boards of beechwood
with the baleful signs . . . .'*—over and over— *'Burn
the boards of beechwood with the baleful signs . . .'*
What does *that* mean?"

From the other side of the lean-to came indications
that even Appledore was engaged on some peradven-
tures of his own on the other side of either the Gates of
Horn or of Ivory. *"Proclaimed!"* he muffled through
his beard and blanket. "Proclaimed is Appledore the
First, Phallus Invictus! —Wench, come here!"

Claud hastily rose him up on his elbow and peered
about in the darkness, but nary wench could he see.
Muttering, he gave his master another nudge. And the
latter said, crisply, "Phmrr!" and rolled over on his
belly. With this had the former daftylad perforce to be
content.

\* \* \* \*

They left early the next morning, with the blessings
of at least two of the Vestal Virgins ringing in their
ears. Appledore, who felt the cold and chill, wet mists,
coughed and blew his nose and hawked his phlegm.

Claud sat huddled and silent. Peregrine saw in his
mind's eye the mysterious and oracular words, *Burn
the boards of beechwood with the baleful signs*—a
phrase concerning which the impromptu prophetess,
Mother Boadicea, had professed herself as baffled as
himself. "But sure," she said, comfortingly, "It
wouldn't be an oracle if 'twere couched in simple
words which any ploughboy could ken straight off.
Depend up on it, me son, whin the time comes, yez'll
be understandin' of it well enough."

"Be quiet," said Claud, of a sudden, though no one
had spoken. "Stop, stop—" they reined in. There was
no sound save the perpetual drip of the mists and dew as
they distilled on leaf and twig of tree and shrub, and fell
to the ground.

After a few moments, Peregrine asked, low, "What,
Claudy?"

"Thought I heard . . . a horn? . . ."

"Perhap was the horns of Elfland," suggested the
old sage, half-wry. At that moment a horn sounded,
and not too very far off in the thick greyness which
moved and crept all about them. Appledore sat open-
mouthed. "Chronos and Old Night!" he muttered.
There was the drumming of hoofbeats, nearer and
nearer. Peregrine spurred his mule up off the path, for
he dared not trust to go down; and his two companions
followed suit.

Hoofbeats, the cries of wild beasts, the sounds of
horns and of voices, nearer and nearer and—
seemingly—from high up—

Said Appledore, "I hope tis not—"

Said Claud, "Oh, tis not, I hope, the—"

"—Wild Hunt, I hope not—" said Perry.

Out of the morning mists, which lay so heavy on the
ground and cloaked the trees and muffled the hills and

vales, there came plunging three huge wisants and an even huger aurochs, heads all flung back and nostrils distended, tongues lolling and foam flying, flanks heaving—from some one of them a gout of blood splashed hot upon Peregrine.

Came men mounted upon horseback, the first with face muffled in cloak out of which there thrust a horn which he wound again and again, and after him three more: one with bow in hand and arrow nocked, and two with lances couched. The hornsman sped right on with his *tru-ru-ru*, perhaps he saw them not; the others slowed and turned dark faces as they flashed by, raised arms and fists—

*"Immanuel!"* halloo'd one.

*"Dulkarnahyeen!"* bellowed the second.

*"Essus!"* shouted the third.

And were gone, for one instant as though they had never been: then from the mists below, following the steep path, came the echoing hoofbeats, the sounds of the horn, the repeated bellowing of the fleeing beasts, and the recurrent shouts of the men.

If men they were, thought Peregrine. Yet said aloud at once, "Save there be new gods in the heavens, this is no wild hunt of theirs—"

"And besides," Claud declared, suddenly brave and forgetful of his prior words, "whoever heard of the Wild Hunt in the daytime?"

"Appledore? Appledore?—Confound that wizard, has he—"

A small rain of falling stones heralded the descent of Appledore, as well as a stream of explanation and apology: The ass would flee, there was no stopping him, he and his master together would surely have been run down and trampled, "Who can hold, my friends, what will away?" and so forth and so on.

Peregrine, interrupting: "Is not Dulkarnahyeen a name for Alexander?"

Appledore, relieved to be on familiar ground: "It is, it is, my Per! And 't means, Of the Twain Horns. For so were he ever named since being proclaimed the son of Ram-Head Ammon—" He stopped, slightly perplexed, turned his wizard-hat round a few times as though by so doing he could screw an answer out of his puzzled pate. "As for Essus, why, hmm, hmm, let me see, surely we have here another exemplum of horns signifying power, for . . . mmm . . . mmm . . . Alexander: Eskander (as the Syrians call him): Eskanderus: Es'k'us: Essus? . . . Eh? . . ." He scanned their faces, his own falling. "No, no," he said. " 'Twill not do, the fetch is too long, by far, and it will not reach, not even Antonius the wordsmith can stretch it far enough to make it fit. Yet, Essus is a horned god, one of the older sort, the true sort, no doubt that Mother Boadicea could tell us something of him, for he is paid honor and faith by the shepherds of the great Isle of Briton—though whether those same shepherds be Celts or Saxo-Angles, I cannot say."

Peregrine shook his head, as though to dislodge a buzz or an earwig, syllables and hoots of horns, horns and echoes . . . "Nay, but one more, wise Appledore. What of Immanuel?"

The Child of Abraxas swayed his rump as he ambled away. The wizard turned his head, and, over his shoulder said, "Perhaps the first syllable should be assimilated into the second, which would give us *manual*—a reference, may it not be, to the Hand of Power? A piercing thought . . . More than that, for now, I know not.—Did all three of those huntsmen look dark, dark to you?"

Gradually the mists were thinning out, yet still the trees ahead wore coats of gauzy grey. "They did. I was brought to mind of Taprobane, or India *extra Gangem*."

Claud said, "Why so far? Are there no dark men in Nubia?"

"And is Nubia so much less far?"

An arrow abruptly terminated their geographical discussions. The *thwack!* which it made in going into the heavy pine tree just ahead of Appledore was emphasized by the thud of the first stone slung, and then by the two next ones— each one hitting a tree near a rider: clearly no mere angry rocks tossed by a rustic, but skillfully aimed and flung by a master slingster.

"Rein up," said Peregrine. In this narrow defile, hemmed in by high hills and higher cliffs, shrouded in concealing trees, of what use was a sword?—or, for that matter, spears? Before either could be had to hand they might all be dead. Not even flight was to be thought of, for the Abraxas-ass when alive had certainly not been bred for speed, and his swaybacked form blocked the trail; moreover, wattled hurdles filled with boulders might very well crown any number of cols ahead, and once those hurdles be slipped, nothing could have saved them from being crushed beneath the avalanche.

So—"Rein up," said Peregrine.

Silently, they awaited instructions not long in coming.

"Dismount," a voice ordered. "And tie your mounts to one tree and then move twenty paces ahead—counting aloud—and so stand still." They obeyed; Appledore, not choosing to plead the natural slowness of age, with soonest haste. A hairy hand relieved Peregrine of his sword, then the same voice said, very near now, "Who gave you leave to hunt in our hills?"

"By your leave," said Peregrine, very civilly, "we have done no hunting here at all."

"By your leave," the same voice said, in a scoffing tone, "allow me to point out that the blood is still wet on your garment."

"Indeed," conceded Peregrine, "the hunt pressed us close as it passed us by—three wisants and an aurochs—but they were not of our hunting. Four dark men—that is, we saw the faces of three of them; the fourth was muffled about the face, and wound a loud, loud horn. Didn't you hear it?"

"Heard it we did, and hastened to find who it was, and, do we find it, we shall know that it was you, despite your plea. —But— 'three wisants and an aurochs'? There are no such great beasts hereabouts, only roe deer and fallow, with now and then a tusky boar. That is a strange tale you tell, and no convincing one."

"Liars strive to tell convincing tales," said Peregrine. "Honest men but tell the truth."

The silence which met his words was broken by another voice. "There is no horn to be found, though, to be sure, they might have cast it away . . . yet I cannot think why they would . . . and more to the point, Caspar, none of the mules and the ass neither, has been sweating. Nor is this one's knife even a bit bloody. Nor are there signs or say of any carcass, no, not so much as a hare's."

There was a sigh. "Turn around, then, if you like," the first voice said. Peregrine liked. He saw Appledore the very picture of feeble old age and unknowing, and Claud once again appearing slack-jawed and daft: but, most to the point, both seeming quite unharmed. He saw, too, a ruddy man with his, Peregrine's own sword, a pale man with a spear, and a small and swarthy man with a sling and a pouchful of stones. He also saw a young woman holding a bow at the ready. To her he chose to make his first knee. "Good day, lady," he said, "and my compliments upon your marksmanship."

First to speak after this was the sallow slingster, and he spoke to Claud, nearest to him. "Got any spare change?" he asked. Claud, after visibly rolling the matter over in his mind, groped in his purse and handed over a single coin, which the other at once bit into in a manner which indicated long habit, not to say expertise. "And if this were any softer," he observed, disgustedly, "I could spread it on my bread, instead of drippings." He held it up and read the inscription, being slightly incommoded by the damage done to it by his own teeth-marks. " *'Sennacherib XXXII, Great King, King of Kings, King of Lower Upper Southeast Central Assyria. One denarius.'* Well, goody. This might just suffice to buy a single sesame seed in a buyer's market. Where'd y' get it?"

"I stole it from a dragon's hoard," said Claud, rather sulkily.

"It must have been a damned small dragon," said the slingman, after considering the comment.

"It was," Claud said, simply.

The comment of the ruddy man was even simpler, and was accompanied by a gesture. "Onward," he said.

\*    \*    \*    \*

They were so high up that they could look down and see hawks soaring. The pale man pointed. "Now, that high pinnacle of rock down there,'' he said, ''or, well, maybe not that one in particular, but one like it . . . overlooking a river such as that—'' his gesture took in the winding silver arc, too far away for any vessels to be made out, ''—on the one hand, and on the other hand, Bart,'' he gestured again, ''overlooking that whole entire valley and yonder pass thereunto . . . say it's as large a yoke of oxing could plow it in a morn's time—''

''Plow what?'' asked red Bart. ''The valley? Cas, you are—''

''Not the valley, no the pinnacle as overlooks the valley *and* the pass *and* the river, well—''

''Plow the *pin*nacle? Best not sleep out no more in full moonlight, Cas, it's done you enough damage, tisk.''

But, doggedly, Cas went on. ''Ahind that yon pinnacle is a bit of land about how big, about big enough to be plowed by a yoke of oxing in a morn's time, so say that'd be for emergency crop, say like in during a siege, say. Or could turn out there to graze such cattle as had been drove up from below. And round about the pinnacle, raise up a great heavy foundation, with the native rock bearing most of the burding. On it sets your ward-house, like it were a castle. And you lets nobody enter said valley or leave said valley or voyage up said river with cargo or voyage down said river with cargo, nor catch no fish in said river, nor plant nor plow no crops in said valley, unlessing they pays unto you a fee. See?''

Bart said, ''Cas, you are a mad impractical dreamer.''

''But it will come to it,'' his friend argued. ''Maybe not in your time and maybe not in my time, but 'twill come to it. Way things are going now,'' he said, gloomily. ''Man can't even observe a chicking lay a clutch of eggs, without he wonders whether she'll be 'llowed to hatch them in peace . . . Way things are going now.''

The girl said, in her husky voice, and Peregrine looked at her, not only for her uncommon comeliness, but because she spoke uncommon seldom, ''True for you, and it wasn't that way in the days of the old time religion, when—''

When first, now, he heard the notes of the hunting-horn, Peregrine thought that some word of hers or something in the air or in the landscape—though land-scape and air alike now different, with the mists gone and the sun shining warmly even through the thinner air, and nothing obscured but all lying clean and open—had, by trick, reminded him of the earlier morning's scene. But in only one second more he realized that all had heard it.

It was, as it swept by, at least the second act of some odd and splendid pageant, and no doubt it made a great deal of sense to its participants: but its human spectators might have been trampled without moving, save for the movements their mouths made in dumbfoundered as-tonishment, had not the mules and donkey of the Sapodillan and the wiry mountain ponies of their *pro-forma* captors had the animal sense to remove themselves—and their riders—from the path of the on-rushing hunt . . . if ''hunt'' it were indeed. For first came the hornblower, and though warm, warm was the hour of day, still had he his face muffled in his cloak; and there was an aurochs; and there were as before three wisants; and three darky men mounted; and for each and every man there was as before a horse; but the combinations were different this time by far.

The man whose loud-sounding horn was thrusting from his muffled mouth, he rode the aurochs. His three fellows sate upon the wisants.

*"Essus Christus!"* cried one.

*"Negro, sed formoso!"* cried the second.

*"Immanuel Dulkarnahyeen!"* cried the third.

And the horses thereof galloped freely following.

And all were gone before an arrow could be loosed or a slingstone slung. And the sounds of horns and hooves echoed and the dust danced and the scattered pebbles rattled and tumbled a moment more. And all lay silent.

*"Behold the Ram of God, Who taketh away the sins of the world."* These words floated on the air and rang in all their ears, but when they came to discuss it all, none knew or could remember who it was who had said them. But, passing up the windy path a bit, there they saw a banneret a-waving in the mild breeze; and on its white background there was Ammon in black. The staff had been plunged into the barm-turf. They looked at it in silence, then Peregrine tugged it up. He shrugged. "I have lacked me a staff and a banner," he observed. "Perhaps this will serve me as well another."

Appledore shook his head at this. "What good thing ever came forth out of Egypt?" he asked. "Best leave it where it was."

But the young man smiled and waved his new ensign in the wind.

*    *    *    *

"In whose name do you guard these woods?" asked Peregrine.

"You might say that we're a quadrumvirate," said the slingster. The fair young woman made a sound which might be written as,

"Hmph!"

"A quadrumvir-et-ux-ate," said the sallow slingster, correcting himself.

"I don't believe I heard your names," Peregrine

said, indicating the slingster and the young woman.

"She's Di and I'm Mel," said Mel.

"I'm Peregrine and this is Appledore and Claud."

"Pleased to meet you."

"Oh, the pleasure is mine. Ours, I mean."

"Good hunting in your native country?" asked Di.

"Sapodilla? Not very, I'm afraid." He was about to give a brief description of how they sometimes hunted wild chickens with throwing sticks, but decided, suddenly, not to.

"Pity," said Di.

"Sapodilla, eh. Last pagan kingdom in Lower Europe," said Bart.

"Yes," said Peregrine. "Oh, some missionaries got through, a few years ago, but when the peasants heard them preaching premarital chastity, they quit listening. The peasants said that no one but a fool or a king would marry a virgin, not knowing if she might prove barren. Besides, they said it was bad luck to get blood on your—" He stopped abruptly, blushed slightly.

"Pity," said Di again; but he was not sure which clause of his conversation she was referring to.

"Yes, well," the reddy man said, "we used to go religious missioning ourselves, but gave that up oh a long time ago; decided that the game wasn't worth the candle. Played a starring role in that scene once, but no more. Sapodilla, hey. Must have been an older brother of yours chanced to come by this way a few years ago, told us somewhat of the scene back there. Looked a bit like you, though blond."

"Blond?" Peregrine's interest was quickened. "That must've been Austin. Where did he go, can you tell me?" Austin, nearest in age, had been his close friend, had promised to send word. But if word he had sent, word had not reached Peregrine.

The path, for a change, now turned downwards. Bart

considered the question. " 'Tell you?' Well . . . we can *show* you—"

But his black-haired companion shook his head. "That would take us too far out of our way, then. Best tell him. —Lad, can you tie a square knot? You can, eh. What's to remember in tying one?"

A bit puzzled, Peregrine found his fingers of their own motion beginning to fiddle with the end of the reins he held. And in a moment the answer came to him. "Right over left, left over right," he said.

"Correct. Well, we leave you here. Steady on as the way goes, and then, lad, remember. And may all good things rightfully to be yours, be yours."

The four waved, nudged their ponies, and, single file, in a second were gone, gone into thick woods along a trail so narrow that an unkeen eye might never have noted it.

"Odd," said Appledore, "very odd. Though, else my magery is worthless, we shall see odder yet, for these be odd times. Ah, well. Let us amble onwards, keeping eyes open and ears a-pricked, and in hopes that the rest of the day shall prove somewhat less exciting. I had a wife once, who—"

"*You* had a wife!" This comment, or, rather, exclamation, came from a figure, until then unperceived who stood by the side of the way leaning on an oddly-shaped length of wood which nevertheless seemed somewhat if vaguely familiar to Peregrine. The man wore a short tunic very much the worse for wear, and his eyes were bloodshot. "*You* had a wife! Listen, strangers, haul up your mounts and moor them to yonder tree, and let me tell you how *I* had a wife once. Moan, natter, sigh, morning till night, 'O do not fear, gallant Ulyxes, come what may I shall ever be faithful to you. After all—*who asked?*

"And if I so much as wanted to go for a little trip night-fishing on the wine-dark sea, why who was that there on the seashore moaning and sniffling and wringing her hands and offering victims for my safe return? Right! 'Listen, Penny, honey,' I'd say, 'I'm only going around the cape to catch a couple of squid,' but did it help! 'O do not fear, gallant Ulyxes, come what may, I shall be faithful to you.' Well, shit . . .

"Finally, I got my chance and beat it off to the wars and, let *me* tell *you*, man, *I* had a *ball*—because those gently-reared daughters of kings, try as you may to teach them, they never really *do* learn what a nice fancy fuck is like. Well, I figure, what the Hell, home is where the hearth is, and after all this time she must have taken at least a *couple* of lovers and learned a few things, no reason to be bashful with *them* the way she always was with me, her lawful husband. So I *go* home . . . and I go incognito . . . and I peer into the lofty hall—and what do I see? Place is what I mean like *jammed* with studs! I say to myself, 'Hot dog!' I figure I'll go back down to the beach, then have myself announced by a herald, and give the studs a chance to split without any embarrassing scenes, and then, well, naturally, there'll be a hot time in the old town tonight!

"But what else do I see, besides all the young bucks? I see my own lawful wedded wife is what I see, and she's up to her old stunt at the loom—I mean, how many times have I said to her, 'Nelly, we got *servants* to do the weaving, doll!'—there she is, the bucks and studs all eating up my groceries and guzzling and gobbling and belching and farting in the hall, instead of teaching her nine and sixty tribal lays in the scented bedchamber, and because why? Because *she's* at her frigging *loom* again, and chanting like a goddamn invocation, 'O never fear, gallant Ulyxes, come what may, I shall ever remain faithful to you!' So says I to myself, neither time nor space nor infinite opportunity—*this* icicle, *nothing* will melt! So I like beat it back to my galley again, and ever since I been sailing back and forth across the dolphin-torn, the dong-tormented sea; and do *you* know what, kids? *I* don't care if I *never* get back to Ithaca; that's about *my* wife, Dad, and now let's hear about yours.''

Appledore slowly bowed his head without unsettling his mantle-cap again, and said, ''Stranger, after a master storyteller, he who has but dull domestic anecdotes to impart had best be silent on the score. But by the sight of that oar on which you lean, O gallant Ulyxes (for such I take to be your name), I would gather that you have nevertheless full tired grown of the dolphin-torn, the dong-tormented sea, and that you intend to travel so far inland that eventually you will chance upon a child who will say, 'O mammy, and what is that oddy thing the stranger-man do tote upon his shoulder?' and, she happening to give such an answer as it might be, 'Babby dear, and peradventure 'tis a pestle for to husk grain,' what time you will settle there and never have to be reminded of ships again.

And the stranger allowed his mouth to open and his bearded jaw to drop and he narrowed his bloodshot eyes and answered, ''You are right. Say, what are you, some kind of a wizard or something? Well, folks, time and tide and all that, and my blessing to you and all of you is, May a faithful, frigid wife ne'er be your portion, and may baleful signs ne'er be inscribed agin you on tablets of beech-wood. Farewell.''

These last words flared up in Peregrine's mind like a gobbet of fat upon a hot ember, and for a full moment he was struck still with astonishment. Then, immediately, he turned upon his saddle and sought the

stranger; then he with no little difficulty turned his mule
and trotted back along the path. And then he began to
call, again and again, "Ulyxes! O gallant Ulyxes! Stay!
Return! And I will give you directions and letters of
introduction to a fair and quiet land where no child
knoweth what an oar may be—"

But all in vain, for the gallant wayfarer and seafarer
had vanished like a pinch of salt in a cauldron of Water.
"And [said Appledore] And 'tis strange, that, in more
ways than only one, for as to his oar, O Aeons! how far
he must have walked from the nearest, let us say, 'The
nearest'?, the nearest seaport or shore—and yet, I
would swear that his oar was still damp and a smelled
briny. Strange, strange, exceedingly strange: Yet
stranger yet may yet befall us."

As to what next befell them, what next befell them
was a file of soldiery emerging from the bosky as the
way curved, and with a crisp cry of, "Halt! In th'
Imperial Name!" several of them seized the bridles of
the beasts, and the rest barred both advance and retreat.
And a centurion stepped forth and demanded, "Proclaim. Proclaim! *Proclaim!*" Peregrine and Claud automatically inclined their heads and swept their hands
towards Appledore. Who, sweeping off his hat and
dismounting, began to proclaim.

He proclaimed Caesar Augustus, Most High and
Most Serene, Imperial Majesty, Rightful and Only
Lawful Wearer of the Purple, and Chaste Champion of
the Sole True Faith, Conqueror of the Barbarians and
Chastiser of False Doctrines, Sebastocrat and Autocrat
and Emperor of the East, the West, and the Center—

Most of the soldiery nodded and nodded and looked
impressed but the centurion was evidently in the mood
for something a shade more precise, at least, for he
demanded, "His Name! Proclaim his name!"

Appledore, nodding the nod and looking the look of one who was getting there, and would get there yet, if not interrupted, chanted, "Proclaimed be his Name in the Choir of the Angels! Proclaimed be his Name in the Choir of the Cherubim! Proclaimed be his Name in the Choir of the Seraphim, as was heard by the Holy Prophet, *'Holy–'* "

An especially pious sergeant-major at this point shouted, in a stentorian voice, "By the numbers! Genuflect! *One!*"

All the soldiers fell upon their right knees.

" *'–Holy–'* "

*"Two!"*

All the soldiers fell upon their left knee as well.

" *'–Holy–'* "

*"Three!"*

All the soldiers crossed themselves.

" 'Lord of Hosts, Heaven and Earth—' "

Someone, evidently the commissary-major, walked up and down, checking out the mules and gear, and making swift notes on a pair of wax tablets with a stylus. And the voice of Appledore went on, "—Immortal, Omnipotent, Omniscient, Omnipresent—" the soldiers still crossing themselves. And on.

And on.

And on.

Eventually he had to pause to swallow, and get his breath. The sergeant-major at once, and by the numbers, got his troop to its feet again. And the commissary-major handed over a handful of talleys to Peregrine, and said, "If your Honor will call upon the nearest Office of the Imperial Treasury, he can exchange these for parchment script which will entitle him to call upon the nearest office of the Imperial

Bursary, where the script will be redeemed in lawfully coined coin of the Realm for the full value at current prices for all beasts and gear, said valuation may be appealed at the nearest office of the Imperial Legate by application and compurgation in triplicate and payment of the requisite fees if not satisfactory to Your Honor, Your Reverence's beast is exempted by Imperial Rescript and as to Your Reverence's gear I do not find any of it listed in the Nomenclature, so pass, friends, in the Emperor's Name—''

Here he paused, as though trying to remember something, and Appledore promptly plugged the gap with, ''Christus Invictus!''

''Christus Invictus!'' said the commissary-major.

''Christus Invictus!'' said the centurion. Appledore bowed and so, after only a second, did Peregrine and Claud.

''Pass!'' said Appledore, to Peregrine, and started off at a fairly rapid clip, twisting the tail of the Child of Abraxas to prevent him from dallying.

''Pass!'' said Peregrine to Claud, and started off at a pace no less rapid.

There was no one for Claud to say, ''Pass!'' to, and the sergeant-major was (he thought) eyeing him in a manner he liked less than not; so to the sergeant-major he said, ''Christus Invictus!'' and set off after Peregrine.

Behind him he heard the sergeant-major bellow, ''By the numbers! One!''

''*Christus!*'' They responded.

''Two!''

''*Invictus!*'' and brought the butt-ends of their spears upon the ground with a crash.

''And rather there, than on *my* butt-end,'' muttered Claud. The sound of the spears being brought to port-arms, followed by the troop reciting the Credo in unison as they counted off and dressed rank, or something, died away behind them.

"Well, we're alive, anyway," said Claud.

Appledore, a trifle nettled, said, "What do you mean, 'anyway'? You're a damn sight better off than merely being alive. If it hadn't been for my presence of mind and a memory like a slippery well, at least one of those spears might be *up* your butt-end and not merely *on* it, to say nothing of—as presently—being nowhere near it."

"Yes, Uncle Appledore," said Claud, contritely.

At this moment a curious thing happened to the way. It not only branched, but one fork of it twisted and turned, and crossed the other by a natural bridge, formed when a stream—now dry—had worn away the softer undersurface of a great rock. Peregrine said, "Hoy!" Appledore looked back.

"What 'Hoy!'?" he asked.

Peregrine gestured. "Forget what they told us back there?"

"*Who*, 'Back there'? *Which*, 'Back there'? The soldiers back there? The sailor back there?"

Peregrine said, " 'Right over left, left over right . . .'?"

Appledore stopped and scanned the topography. "By the God," he conceded, "the boy is right. It *does* go 'right over left.' Well. And what about it? What lies thataway?"

"Austin lies thataway. That is, at least, Austin *went* thataway."

"And what about *that?*"

Peregrine turned and began to climb. "Nothing about that, to you, then. He isn't your brother. My thanks to you, Doctor Appledore, Sagus Invictus, and I wish you good fortune on your own journey, wherever you go.''

Claud scratched his head, hestitated, then started after Peregrine. Appledore shrugged, began to ride on, then stopped, then swore softly, then turned round his beast. "Ah, well," he said, "I've nothing against following whither Austin went. He was a goodly lad, as I recall, though perhaps a mite prone to playing of tricks upon his elders . . . I will not say, 'betters' . . . and it might as well be one way as another. Three heads are better than one, as Cerberus was once heard to howl.''

The way was narrow and tricky under foot, and they all kept their eyes on the ground for a while. And when they lifted them, lo, there the path forked, with one branch of the fork twisting and turning and crossing the other by a natural bridge, formed when a stream—now dry—had worn away the softer underside of a great rock.

"Now, what the Hades,'' grumbled Appledore. "Are we back where we were before, only—?'' He paused and scratched his head.

But Peregrine merely repeated, a trifle doggedly, " '—left over right,' '' and started to climb again, Claud following, with no more than a puzzled grunt.

"Bide a bit,'' warned the sage. "There may be a spell involved here—Bide, I say—''

"Spell or not, knot or not, if Austin went thisaway, then thisaway I go too.'' And so they went, and this time without a repetition. The way soon widened into a road, and the road showed a few signs of having been paved, then more than a few, and at once became a broad highway set with blocks of stone, and it passed beneath an arch. And from the far side of the arch came a troop of men, one of whom bore an oar and another of whom bore a length of rope. And behind them, con-

cealed by the arch and visible only in shadow, were the
shadows of several other men, whose arms did not
swing free.

"Halt, in th' Imperial Name!"

Before Appledore could open his mouth, Claud, in
his most rustic accent, said, with a gesture, "Brudder,
and what be dat oddy ting which de stranger-man do
tote upon he shoulder?"

Peregrine at once answered, "Why, Brudder, dat I
do not know, save and unless it be's a sort of pestle for
to husk grain. Hey, Uncle?"

Some of the troop guffawed, Appledore shaking his
head and looking not merely ignorant, but senile as
well. And the Chief Petty Officer said, "One Hell of a
lot of use would *you* be to th' Imperial Navy, and you
may lay to that. Pass, bumpkins."

They this time did not merely pass, they skedaddled,
moving as awkwardly as possible, and bumping into
one another. Behind, the voice said, "Let's weigh
anchor. I knew this was a hare-brained scheme, setting
up a press-gang at the city gate, far side. Waste one
morning, and what do we see? Three single-voyagers
with hangovers, which we sling up, though fat lot o'
use they'll prove, I warrant; and one old gaffer on a
jackass, plus his two nevvews as don't know a oar from
their orifices."

"Aye-aye, Chief. Arright, Chief."

"*Hawp, arreep, heep, hawp!*" The press-gang took
one turn of the main street, and the three others made
sure to take another. "That was well-done, lad," said
Appledore. "And I was not, myself, about to do more
than to commence another Proclaiming, without even
stopping to think that no one had asked me to."

Peregrine said, "Yes, Claud. What gave you the
idea?"

Claud disdained even modesty. "Needn't have gone to sea to have heard about press-gangs," he said. And with that they all, including the Child of Abraxas, came to a sudden halt and looked at each other; and then they looked around them, at the nets hanging up here and there, at the slops-shops, and they lifted up their heads and sniffed the briny air. And then looked at each other again.

"Well, and may I never," muttered Appledore. "And, well, that may indeed account for the still dampy oar of Ulyxes. But, may I ask, what will account for the presence of a seaport where of rights there ought to be no sea? True, certain ancient geographers, including those who wrote an history of the Argonauts, did declare and affirm that the Danube flowed into the Adriatic, but we be . . . we were . . . we ought to have been, are, were, should, shite and leeks!—as far from the one as the other—"

Peregrine straightened his neck. "Be that all as it may be," he said. "I am not one to quarrel presently with the inscrutable decrees of the Fates. Let us get us onward, then, being thankful that the commissary-major's requisitions have left us our personal gear . . . Ho, stranger, can you direct us to the Imperial Treasury?"

The man so hailed, a civil-looking fellow in early middle-age, eyed them with mild curiosity, said, "Certainly, sir, if you have no more pleasant way of wasting your time. Go straight down the Way till you come to the Theater, opposite which stands the Cathedral, formerly the Temple of an Abomination, and turn left till you are facing the Pro-Cathedral, formerly the Temple of another Abomination. Here you will find yourself facing what was formerly The Baths, scene of simply undescribable scenes of nakedness and other lecheries, but now purified and the Imperial Treasury. And may I wish you joy of whatever fool's errand and useless quest takes you thither: If you are well, I am well, and it is well." And with that he passed on.

"Hmmm," said Appledore. "One has the impression that he is somehow not persuaded of the fiscal integrity of the current Reign. Perhaps we should simply forget it and get a dram to drink. That journey has made my throat and tongue resemble something from the interior of Lower Libya, and during a drought, too."

"Suit your own pleasure, but those were good mules, and Sapodilla's second-best armor and so forth is equal to other places' first-best, and sometimes better. I owe it to my Dadda and our native realm to salvage what we can, because we may be needing every penny we can get for something more essential than wine."

Claud, who had been listening with an only semi-revised version of his original slack-mouthed, half-wit look, brightened at this last reference. "Whores, you mean?"

"When in Rome," Peregrine said, simply, and, hoisting his saddle-bag, started off, accompanied by Claud, and followed, after no very long pause, by Appledore.

An old man thrust out a skinny paw at them. "Have pity, my sirs," he whimpered, "upon a former heathen priest once lapped in the finest wool and supplied with silver and gold by the deluded, but now, after having seen the light and accepted Christian baptism, content with holy poverty, seeking only the merest modicum on which to subsist during the certainly not more than a few days remaining to him in this vale of tears and illusion: and your petitioner will ever pray for you, whenas on high. Give something."

Peregrine withdrew the smallest coin he could find, and, the converted priest grabbing for it with something which did not seem precisely like Christian resignation, withdrew it a bit. "This is yours," said Peregrine, "if you can advise me what to do with all these"—here he showed him the clutch of talley-sticks.

The oldster uttered an unseemly cackle. "You might use them for kindling," he suggested. Then, bethinking him that this would earn no alms, hastily assumed a more serious look, and said, "Ah, my young sir, hard upon the side of the Treasury, formerly The Baths, a scene of frenzies debilitating to more than the merely physical health in times gone by, you will observe a group of sundry citizens gathered there to discuss Sacred subjects such as Divine Theology. Enquire there for Cornelius the Cappadocian; meanwhile, forget not—Ah, thank you, thank you!" and he leapt and catched the coin with a degree of limberness which might have indicated that in his unregenerate youth he had cast many a discus though alas probably in a condition of heathen bare-assedness: woe.

Stains upon the marble of the building they sought and finally found testified—though the letters which had caused the stains had long since either fallen or been ripped off—testified that The Baths had been the gift of a public-spirited citizen named P. Mendipidudus Something-or-other, or something like that, as a memorial to The Divine—but here zeal had hacked away the Imperial Name and stone, effacing more than that mere hint of former heathenry. And, sure enough, hard by the side of the building, was a group of citizens engaged in an intense, though low-voiced discussion of what must surely have been Divine Theology.

As the three approached, one of the citizens, a wall-eyed fellow with a pot belly, hissed something, and the conversation ceased immediately. And began almost at

once, after the citizens had swiftly scanned the newcomers, in a rather louder tone.

"Assuredly," said one of them, "The Father and the
Son, Substance and Essence," he said, noncommit-
tally.

"And the Holy Spirit," added a third; but as to the
procession of that Spirit, he carefully said nothing.

"What deed of Christian kindness and of corporal
or, better yet, of spiritual mercy, may we do for you,
strangers as I perceive you all to be," enquired the
squinter. Peregrine held forth the talleys. The wall-
eyed man disdained to partake of the guffaw which
united his fellows. "Ah, to be sure, to be sure," he said
reflectively. "Now, there is only one man who can be
of help to you in this matter, and as the Treasury
—formerly The Baths, and a dreadful scene these latter
must have been, to hear tell, multitudes concerning
themselves with a merely physical cleansing, regardless of the filthy states of their unregenerate and certainly damned souls—mind you, I speak but by hear-
say, having had the good fortune to have been born into
a godly family in my native Cappodocia, where—"

"Speak no more," said Peregrine, "for you must
certainly be that Cornelius of whom I have heard mention. Assist us, I pray, and you will certainly not find us
ungrateful."

It was probably doubtful if they could have found
their way, unguided, through the vast and only partly-
ruinous complex which had once housed The Baths,
provincial structure though it was. And, thought Peregrine, if it had been full of all the money there was
room for, rich indeed would have been whoever currently Caesar was in that particular area of the Central
Roman Empire; but the only sign of usage which he was
able to observe was in the one room whose pool still

held water, and here—the broken roof admitting sunshine—an industrious Armenian was raising live carp for the Friday market. However, there were ample signs, such as here an office outfitted with all the needful equipage, and there a stack of tablets, and elsewhere a wall covered with cabinets of which the pigeon-holes were full of papyrus record-rolls—all, all covered with loops of dusty cobwebs—that once, at least, after the building had ceased to function as a bath it had for a while at least functioned as, it might be, a treasury.

But, unless the bats which hung in clusters on the walls, and the rats which scuttled away from the clutters of ruined documents in the halls, unless these creatures themselves might be deemed to hold treasures of a sort, it functioned so no longer.

At length they found themselves in a vaulted chamber a deal less dusty than the others, and there, surrounded by well-ordered stacks of tablature and rolls of papyrus which seemed comparatively clean, they observed an elderly man, himself of only slightly dusty appearance, who was chanting aloud from an Apocryphal Gospel. He looked up, briefly, without ceasing his encantation, and as this seemed to bid fair to continue forever, Peregrine began impatiently to rattle the few small coins which he still had in his hands upon the chance of meeting yet another useful beggar.

''—and in the Name of the Father and of the Son and of the Holy Spirit, aeons without number, *sator arepa*, what can I do for you gents?'' inquired the clerk, placing an embroidered bookmark in his codex, and rising and coming forward briskly enough for one of his age and stiffness.

''This is the office of the Imperial Treasury dealing with the redemption of talley-sticks given in exchange for beasts and gear and armor, weaponry, and such, such having been commandeered in the Imperial Name *vice* the commissariat-major, is it not, Menander Protector?'' asked Cornelius the Cappadocian.

Menander Protector smiled a thin smile, and began to rub his scrawny mitts together. ''Certainly, certainly, under the terms of Imperial Rescript LXCVII, An. MCVI, sub. cap. ut. fut. CCCXXVVVIII,'' he said, ''Next!''

Peregrine, nudged, stepped forward and handed over his bundle of talley-sticks. The ancient clerk nodded, rummaged in a vast chest rather like a second-hand sarcophagus of the unregenerate times, came up with another bundle of similar sticks, and set to work matching them: at length found the proper matches, notch for notch and slit for slit. Then he began to peer at the parchment tags attached to the office set. ''Well, well, these seem all in order,'' he said, at length, satisfied. And, putting them down, he began to walk back to his chair and his book.

''Hoy!'' said Peregrine. The clerk waved his hand. ''Do not be impatient, young man,'' he urged. ''All in good time. As soon as I have finished the next chapter of this quasi-canonical text—though I have little doubts but that the next synod or Council will admit them to full canonicity—I shall make the necessary and official entries into the proper set of tablets.''

Cornelius nudged Peregrine, and gave him a look. To follow the look from its source in the Cappadocian's eyes was a task which might have baffled Archimedes and taxed Euclid, but it seemed to Peregrine, going more by intuition than by pure mathematics, that the look was directed and had reference to the hand of his which held the money. He emptied it upon the marble counter with a clatter, exclaiming, under his breath, ''Christus Invictus!''

At once the ancient clerk Menander spun about on his boney heel. "Christus Invictus!" he echoed. "And, observing you to be a youth of unquestionable piety and doubtless purity of doctrine, and may I not as well attend to your duties immejitly, thus releasing you from this material and illusory world the sooner to attend vespers at the Pro-Cathedral, formerly the Temple of an Abomination." And, muttering to himself, he set to copying the inscriptions of the papyrus tickets attached to the office set of the talley-sticks into an enormous set of tablets; in the course of which task the heap of coins somehow disappeared without sound or trace.

"Done and done and done!" he declared at last, looking up, brightly. "And now do you be off to your orisons and I back to my book. Ahah and hahah, had I but followed both orisons and books in my youth's entirety to the complete exclusion of clerkwork, might I not by now have gained a martyr's crown? or at least a bishopric? Eheu; observe, young man, the lesson implicit. Fare thee well."

But Peregrine, owing no doubt to his essentially pagan nature, said, "But what of the parchment scrip which we are to change for coin of the realm at the Imperial Bursary?"

The old man raised his eyebrows at this; but still stayed his retreat. "The parchment scrip? Well, well, perceive the as yet undiminished fire of youth, too often allowed to run unrestrained and thus become mere carnality. Other young men—I have certainly no reference to a godly one such as yourself—*other* young men would no doubt be all afire to obtain their coin, and for what? Not merely for the forbidden purpose of laying up treasure on earth, but for the equally condemned purpose of squandering the aforesaid coin in the multitude of brothels and winecellars with which this insufficiently Christian city alas abounds; little do they reck, as they pay monies to the probably pagan harlots to strip them of their already insufficient clothing in order to perform sundry fornications upon them—'' Claud at this point began to move restlessly from one foot to another, Peregrine sighed, and even the elderly Appledore was observed to twitch a little bit. ''—of the Hell-fire which certainly awaits them; avoidable, however, by a sufficient repentance, *mmff*, want your parchment scrip do you?''

His hands rested, palms upright, upon the marble counter in what might possibly have been an attitude of prayer. Cornelius the Cappadocian seemed to be pointing one eye at Menander and the other at Peregrine, and he cupped his paunch in his hands and his lips moved soundlessly. Soundlessly, but intelligibly. Peregrine dipped his hand into his pouch once again, and something clinked briefly before being snapped up.

''Ah woe is me and what is this?'' the aged M. Protector stared, aghast. ''A coin bearing the image of an Abomination, the name of which shall not pass my lips. Though undoubtedly made of a pure silver, so blind were they in ancient days to a true sense of values: sound money and false gods—'' This seemed not to promise well for a good conclusion to Peregrine's quest for coin of the realm, but he was loath to abandon his search now.

''I shall hide it from sight, lest its so-called beauty tempt some poor soul, and tonight will carry it to a Christian silversmith to have it melted down, and so put an end to the possibility of harm. Well, well, and so back to my—''

Peregrine said, firmly, ''The scrip. The parchment—''

''Exactly,'' said Menander Protector. ''Where is it?''

"Where is *what?*"

"The parchment, wherewith I am to indite the scrip."

"You mean that—" began Peregrine.

"I should have thought, worthy Menander Protector," said Appledore, speaking for the first time, "that the one thing an Imperial Office would not lack would be parchment."

A smirk passed over the old clerk's face. "Then you would have thought wrong!" he announced, triumphantly. "It is not the duty of this Office to furnish parchment for applicants. This, they must furnish for themselves. And, should you doubt me, I refer you to the decision in the case of *Theme of Bythinia vs. Estate of the Protopresbyter of Cyrenaica et al.*, XXXth Book of Constitutions, Liber VVVXXXCCCIII, par. III."

Perhaps by this time even Cornelius the Cappadocian was growing a trifle impatient, not, surely, out of any mere carnal lust, such as did indeed seem to be affecting Claud with an internal flame and ichorous itch, but doubtless to be gotten back to his discussions of Sacred Theology with the citizens outside. He cleared his throat with a phlegmy effort. "The learned, pious, and diligent prothonotary Menander Protector is as usual, correct," he said. "However. When I inform him that these three applicants have come at great effort and great cost from far away in order to visit the shrine of the Virgin and Martyr Euphemia, she who, have for sixteen months by day and by night repulsed the vile attentions of the unregeneratively heathen her husband, Casimir the Carpathian, until in a fit of heathen rage he slew her by his sword with a several many smites, and have moreover willingly given up their wordly effects—most of them, anyway—to the Army of Caesar, which is the Army of Christos Pantocrator after all; no doubt in view of these extenuating circumstances the learned, pious, and diligent prothonotary Menander Protector may not be unwilling, of his own mere free will and kindness, to go look and see if there may not be some old parchment which has outlived its original usefulness; for which purpose the three applicant pilgrims will place a charitable donative into the hands of the prothonotary himself,'' and he said all of this, very, very, fast.

And in a shorter time than by then he would have believed it possible, Peregrine and his comrades and skilled intermediary Cornelius the Cappadocian, were back outside the Treasury building. The afternoon was grown late, but, compared to the insufferable dimness which by now reigned inside the former Baths, it seemed bright. Peregrine turned over the strips of parchment to see what was on the back of the scrip redeemable at the Bursary, for the old clerk had ripped a sheet from an even older book, after exacting from them all a promise that they were on no account to look at the obverse.

''It seems to be from something called *The Entire Art of Making Love, with Illustrations*—But the illustrations are all gone, why that dirty old man!''

''No doubt,'' said the wall-eyed Cappadocian, ''he did it to save your immortal souls. And, speaking of which, may I point out to you that in the adjacent street yonder there are to be found no less than six churches, all formerly Temples of various Abominations, as well as four chantries, a monastery, ten taverns, fifteen wine-cellars, and twenty-five brothels?''

Even Appledore seemed a trifle dazed.

''Twenty-five?'' he repeated.

''Twenty-five. Is it not abominable?''

''It is more than abominable. It is superfluous.''

Here and there oil-lamps had begun to twinkle. The

good smell of supper cooking came wafting through the evening air, along with the thick scent of incense. Hawkers called their wares, the musical bonk-bonk-bonk of wooden bell-boards announced vespers, and, over and above it all, a young woman, obviously dead to all shame, leaned out of a first story window. She had on a very lowcut dress, and she had a cithern in her hands, and she began to strum and to play and finally to sing a love-song.

"Well," said Peregrine, shifting his saddle-bags and hitching up his belt and starting off into the street adjacent, "I guess we'll just have to skip the churches, the chantry, and the monastery."

# PART
# 3

The services of Cornelius the Cappadocian did not
come exactly cheap. However, there were always ex-
tras being added at, he assured them, no extra charge.
He had discovered in the course of conversation in what
was either the seventh or the eleventh winecellar vis-
ited, for example, that Peregrine's paternal grandfather, King Cumnodorius (commonly called King
Cuckold, for reasons which will not escape those having any knowledge of the reputation of his Consort),
had once signed a perpetual treaty of peace with Rome
which had actually lasted an entire year, almost as long
as the reign of the Caesar he had signed it with—on
discovering this, Cornelius at once coupled it with the
circumstance of Peregrine's having lost his sword to the
commissary-major; and darted into the street. Where,
by the happy benevolence of Providence, he met with
Menander Protector coming from Divine Liturgy at the
Crypt of the Martyr. Menander, who doubled as Com-
missioner for Oaths, was persuaded to enter a strictly
private room in the dram-cave, there to take a little wine
for his stomach's sake and for his often infirmities; and
there, also, to issue Peregrine a license to carry a sword
within the city limits.

And so, the next morning found them, after some hot
barley-water (a specific for over-indulgence—or, for
that matter, indulgence), which did nothing to dispel all
the hot memories of the previous night's merry anticks,
at the establishment of one Ulrich, a dealer in slightly-
used metallurgies.

"I knew it, I knew it!" the dealer declared on first

sight of them. He rubbed his bald-spot. "Something
told me when I heard the gate squeak. 'Northerners,' I
said to myself. 'Northerners, coming for a broken
sword, early though it may be for the broken sword
season to have begun.' "

Peregrine was slightly interested by this. "Oh, do
you have broken swords?" he asked. "What do Northerners always want with them?" he inquired.

"Listen," said Ulrich, "Do *I* have broken *swords?!*
I gotta pile o' broken swords as high as my head,
biggest goddam stock of broken swords in the Central
Roman Empire, and every year, as soon as the ice
breaks up on the Wherever-it-is, them crazy norskies
come flocking down with their flocking 'Oh, have you
got a broken sword which my fair eldergodmother
promised if I could find a dwarf who could forge it
again, blah blah blah,' see, I perceive that although
strangers you are, norskies you are not, so freely I can
speak. —'Do I have broken swords?' you ask. Go out
there—you see the pile? Take your pick. I sell 'em by
weight, no promises made as no questions asked or
answered. Take your pick. But lemme warn ya. *No
spells!*

"Dwarfs I don't supply," he added, as though wear-
ily struck by an afterthought.

Negotiations were commenced for an allegedly
damascene blade allegedly owned by an elderly aedile
who was guaranteed to have worn it only for triumphs,
and the Cappadocian, as though honor bound, engaged
in a great deal of bargaining. But Ulrich, after having
indifferently come down a gold piece, merely yawned
and gazed at them all through his heavy-lidded eyes; so
that Peregrine, in whose opinion the blade was well
worth the price, abruptly terminated the cheapening.

"A sensible young fellow," said Ulrich. "A receipt you wouldn't need. My word is my receipt."

"I don't want a receipt," said Peregrine. "All I want is, for good measure, and to seal the bargain, that you throw in a broken sword because whilst my funds are limited, your account has piqued my interest."

Ulrich nodded the nods of the long-suffering. " 'Piqued his interest,' he says. Some got the name, whereas others play the game. All right, goatling. Take your pique of the gebrokeners. No limit on the number of pieces, all I ask and expect is that when laid out before me they should form a recognizable pattern of a sword of normal length and normal breadth."

Appledore, meanwhile, had made himself free of some tattered codices, and Claud was contemplating a cutlass which Peregrine expected shortly to be asked to buy; so he found himself quite alone as he surveyed the pile of broken swords, though aware from time to time of the dealer's expressionless countenance peering out from the window in his office-shed. Most of the broken blades were just so much old iron. Here and there a fragment of what looked like a good blade appeared, but almost never could he discern enough other fragments to make it appear worth the efforts of even the cheapest dwarf. And then something seemed to flash at him, then was gone as he moved toward the place whence it had twinkled.

With hands and feet alike he turned and tugged at aged weapons which had shed man's blood in the four corners of the old earth, then, without his being aware of even touching it, a hilt seemed simply to roll at his feet. And flashed. It was broken. That was to be expected. But he observed, even before his fingers reached it as he stooped, that the design on it represented two serpents copulating, and in the corner of one empty eye-socket he saw a tiny fragment of a shattered gem-stone. And this had been, doubtless, what had flashed at him. Thoughtfully, he picked it up. And thoughtfully he recommenced his search.

"Found what you want? or think you want?" asked Ulrich.

Peregrine set down the broken bits in the rough semblance of a sword. "All right," said the dealer. "But it'll never fly. Close the gates as you go out, please, the element they got coming to this neighborhood nowadays—Goths, Avars, Scythians—even a broken sword wouldn't be safe pretty soon."

The cutlass changed hands, and this time the loose pages of the codex, no even partially entire original being found, were thrown in for good measure. "I thought to beguile my spare moments by attempting to riddle them," was Ulrich's only comment as he acceded to Appledore's request. "But what spare moments, where spare moments? Listen, you think I lick honey in this rotten business?"

The Cappadocian suddenly remembering something left behind at the metallurgical-remnants dealer's—"A trifle, not worth your return, I shall meet you farther on, or assuredly at the inn if not, hard by the side of the Imperial Treasury," he said—the three were quite alone in the quiet street when Peregrine showed them the hilt of the broken sword more closely and with an air quite different from that assumed when at the scrap-yard. "What think you?" he asked.

"This is assuredly," the sage mage began.

"Enough of your assured uncertainties," said Claud, who had even stopped swishing his cutlass proudly, for all the world a boy with a new toy. "The only *assuredly* is that 'twas this same design as was upon the case wherein lay the crown discovered in the dragon cave, is all. Conceal it, master deary, do!'' And so, Appledore rapidly bobbing his head up and down in agreement, this Peregrine made haste to accomplish.

"However," said the older man, "I perceive a certain intimation that I don't know my business, merely because I displayed a certain latitude of opinion in regard to the provenance of the crown—and a good fortune to all of us that the Nomenclature of the commissary-major mentioned neither pods of musk nor measures of barley-meal, Caesar's men being fed never on any grain but wheat; else we had not retained that sack which contained the crown as well . . . where was I? I 'gin to dither, me think me. Ah!''

They had passed out into a sort of square fairly full of people making their way, or simply sitting in the sun. Appledore accosted one of the latter, and, as though picking up the thread of an interrupted conversation, he said, "And you were telling me that the abominable heresy termed Ophiolatry was quite put down in this city—''

"I was not!" the citizen exclaimed. "Just because there haven't been any prosecutions for it of late? Wait till this new government gets settled in; *then* you'll see!''

"I shall? We shall, I mean. Excellent. Ah, young fellows, can you direct me—'' and he pattered along with his two companions as though he had never seen them before; then, approaching someone even older than himself, and slow of step, declared, "Man back there was saying there'll be some prosecutions soon for Ophiolatry, he says, Eh?''

The oldster displayed his withered gums. "Shouldn't be surprised one bit," he affirmed. "Had some cases of it not a lustrum ago. Or was it a double-decade? Memory's not what it was, y'see, I was born the year the plague struck Ravenna, and—''

"You are right, you are right!" Appledore exclaimed. "It was *Ravenna*, not Vienna." And he threw a look both inane and triumphant upon Claud and Peregrine, and they all stepped briskly along. *"Now* let's see," Appledore muttered, under his breath.

Coming towards them was a slightly seedy, slightly furtive man with the look of an unfrocked anchorite. To him Appledore said, "Is it true, Citizen of this City, that, despite the prosecutions of not a lustrum, or was it a double-decade ago, the curious cult called Ophiolatry still survives herein?"

The man leapt as though stung by a vengeful bee, and his chops flapped as he declared, "It is false, sir! I assure you, entirely false! No such traces continue, and those few survivors have all recanted and become as staunch in the Faith as . . ." His voice ran down, and he gazed at Appledore, and then at Peregrine and at Claud. "Why do you ask?" he inquired, low-voiced.

"Hem," said Appledore. "We are strangers, travellers from an antique land. There are a one or two things which we might like to discuss with you, an you could spare us the time. Whither is your dwelling-place?"

His dwelling-place was on the other side of Tannery Row, a foul-smelling area of open vats and sheds where hides lay stinking in pickle, or were turned in tubs with doves' dung, or stretched on fleshing boards to be scraped with special knives. After passing through with open mouths, less from astonishment than from fear of smelling more of the stench than they could safely hope to endure, the travellers found themselves in some open fields of fairly wide extent; at the end of this a lane bordered with old and massive trees, some stooping from very age; and along this way, behind a wall, through a court, and alongside a wool warehouse, was the dwelling-place of Eugenius the Eddessan, their guide and host.

He closed and treble-barred the gate, and set loose the fierce dogs. He locked the door of the house behind them, and closed and fastened the shutters. He took them into an inner room, set a pan against the door (howsoe'er he slid the bolt) and on top of this another pan. Then he came quite close to them, and in a voice so low it was almost a whisper, he asked what they had to discuss with him. Peregrine disclosed the hilt of the broken sword. The man's face slid long, his mouth made the shape of an omicron, and then he said, but still low, "Ah and ah and oh! It is none other than the Serpent-Sword of the Kings of the Ephts, woe art thou, O Ephtland!" and he began to weep silently, and to beat his bosom, though muffling it with his cloak's folds so as to conceal the sound . . .

"Woe art thou, O Ephtland!" continued Eugenius, after wiping eyes and nose, "And woe is thy Serpent-Tower, woe thy Serpent-Column, and . . . and . . ." But here his voice failed him.

"And woe thy Serpent-Crown?" suggested Pere-grine, intending only helpfulness and sympathy. Instantly astonishment, outrage and alarm flashed upon the man's tear-beslubbered face. "There was no such crown!" he exclaimed. "What Serpent-loving man is there who knows not the true description of the crown of the Kings of the Ephts?"

Peregrine strove at once to abate his alarm. It was too late to abate his suspicion, but dissimulation could in no event have been carried much further. "We can offer you," he whispered, "something much better than any mere description. We can offer you," he said, significantly, "a sight of the very crown itself . . . .

"And what," he next asked, after allowing this to sink in, "what can you offer *us?*"

\* \* \* \*

Claud was later on to grumble, "Well, so what of it if he didn't have no daughters nor no servant-girls? He could of bought a one or two, couldn't he?"

\* \* \* \*

Eugenius of Eddessa was in part incredulous, in part overjoyed, in part terrified and in part . . . a very large part . . . didactic.

" 'Ophiolators,' they term us!" he said, scornfully. "Or Ophites, Ophians, or Naasenes. Snake Worshippers! Do they worship their sacred pictures, signs, relics, symbols? Oh perish forbid, ignorant catechumen, they said to me; we do but venerate them. Even so. 'Tis so well-known that serpents are wise, so say their very Gospels, though sadly distorted otherwise. 'Be ye wise as serpents,' eh? They seek the deep, and deep is knowledge. Eh? And does not wisdom lie in the marrow of the backbone and do not these marrows become serpents, gliding from the tomb? Why, of course! So has the Holy Trinity devised it, and by the Holy Trinity, what do I mean? Why what can I mean save the Holy Trinity, videlicet First Man, which is to say, Universal God, and Second Man, the begetter and the only begetter of Christ which is the Third Man, not however being the Third Person of the Holy Trinity, which Third Place is occupied by First Female, id est She-the-Holy-Spirit, clept by some Sophia; no? And First Man conceived Second Man and Second Man begat Third Man and from Third Man and First Female

came Sparks of Light and from Sparks of Light
Quenched in the Supernal Fluids came Dregs of Matter
and from Dregs of Matter came Ialdabaoth and Demiurgos on the one hand and Spirit Soul, alias Serpent,
on the other hand, as well as untold multitudes of Aeons
and other Powers and against all these cometh Second
Sophia the Sister of the Christ whom some say is
Prunicos and there are those who will admit that
Prunicos was Eve and others who, sunken in darkness,
will and do deny it, but can it be denied that Adam, or
Fourth Man, attempted to deny the Serpent, whenas he
fell from Grace, but Grace, who is Sophia, who is
Prunicos, fighting valiantly against the subtle and
sullen Demiurgos and Ialdabaoth, sent Christ from
Heaven to be incarnate in the Pure Vessel to wit the
body of Jesus, and so now see and do behold Jesus
preaching and performing and doing wonders and
miracles and making manifest the Glory of the Serpent
which symbolizes wisdom and as wisdom is holy so is
the serpent holy, being Holy Wisdom, and after the
earthly vessel which was Jesus was lifted upon the
Cross—as the Serpent of Moses was lifted in the
wilderness—there came Christ from Heaven with
Prunicos His Spouse and revived and resurrected Jesus,
who has never died since but goeth about from place to
place undergoing fresh persecutions and at the same
time working fresh miracles, now is this not all perfectly clear?''

Said Appledore, the only one of the three visitors
now capable of speech, ''It is more than clear. It is
obvious.''

Eugenius raised his hands and eyes and made a
sinuous gesture which, Peregrine was later to learn,
was the Sign of the Snake. ''And yet this Doctrine,
clear as crystal, and seeking only the salvation of man-

kind from the Dregs of Matter, is today everywhere persecuted, isn't that incredible? Only in Ephtland was it received with open arms, and of Ephtland and its illuminated Kings and Sword and Crown, I need not speak," and he went on to speak interminably about Ephtland and its illuminated Kings and Sword and Crown, until—

"Hark!" cried Claud, who, failing to derive even the faintest glimmer of interest from the gnostical philosophy as set forth then and there, and having his senses still attuned to the Dark World of Illusion and of Dregs of Matter, had perceived that not all was well in the courtyard. "Hark! Your dogs!"

And, indeed, the dogs had set up a most beastly barking and the sounds of their bodies, as they fell, thudding to the ground, after leaping up against who knew what, at length penetrated even the awareness of Eugenius, Appledore, and Peregrine.

"Hark!" said Eugenius, somewhat redundantly. "The dogs! I am suspicious but that we may have been followed, not to say pursued. Howsomever, a life spent largely as a furtive fugitive has prepared me for all this, and I have become wise as serpents, and where do serpents go when seeking refuge? Exactly." And, so the whole time saying, he had been moving his hands upon the surface of the wall, which wall now slid both backwards and inwards, disclosing a passageway. The Eddessan picked up a tiny oil lamp and, with a genteel "After you," gestured his guests into the cavity and declivity, and they saw the wall return behind them. And all sound ceased.

*   *   *   *

It was fortunate that their guide had supplied the small lamp with oil before beginning his discourse, for the way underground was long and winding, and, in-deed, Peregrine had some notion that the tunnel was perhaps intended to represent some giant serpent. He could not prevent a groan when a gust of wind blew the guttering lamp-wick into blackness, but, in a moment, at about the same moment as he realized that winds do not blow in underground passageways, he lifted up his eyes and saw overhead the glittering stars, and in his nostrils was the scent of dampness and not the dank dampness of the underworld, but the dampness of riv-ers, sounds, streams, estuaries, lakes, ponds, creeks, canals, and other waterways.

"It should be right about here," muttered Eugenius. "Ahah. It *is* right here, thanks to Holy Wisdom, and Her First Born Son, the Snake. I assume that you are all aware of how to handle yourself in a coracle."

There was a long silence at this assumption, broken finally by Appledore, who said, slowly, "Well, I did at one time in my youth, when pursuing some post-graduate studies among the Druids of Northwest Gaul—"

"Yes, they don't make bad coracles there in North-west Gaul," Eugenius agreed, his tone now very matter-of-fact. And somehow, by this time, they had all crept and clambered aboard the craft, of skins stretched upon a framework of wicker. Peregrine was faintly glad that it was night and the moon at present obscured, for he had a notion that this was something like taking passage on the inside of a soap-bubble. Water was not only heard gurgling beneath the bottom, water could be *felt* gurgling beneath the bottom.

"Breathe as little as possible," Appledore counsel-led firmly. "And, please, nobody sneeze . . ."

"Enough of these vanities and pusillanimities," said Eugenius. "Let us commend ourselves to the care and mercies of the Great Serpent who encircles the world in the form of the Ocean Sea. Here goes,'' and he plunged in his paddle and the coracle 'gan to skip and swirl and dart and dangle and bob and leap from wave to wave. ''Take that line there, to portside,'' said Eugenius, crisply, and, when no one obeyed, in part because no one could figure how to determine port from starboard on an almost perfectly circular vessel, he, with a hiss worthy of a serpent-venerator, seized hold of it himself, and in a trice had swung himself out of the coracle. A cry of alarm arose, was at once stifled as the half-moon swung up and out from wherever it had been hiding, and showed the outline of a larger vessel, and someone—presumably Eugenius—still holding the coracle against this vessel's hull.

Peregrine, afterwards, was not quite sure how he had managed to manage his half-stiffened and half-trembling limbs. He thought that perhaps he had levitated.

The vessel was rank with the smell of sheep-fells and wool, and fortunate for the landlubbers that it was so, for more than once they tripped and fell, and had they not fallen upon fells and fleeces and upon bales of wool, their shins would have testified, with scars and scrapes, to their ineptitude.

''The tide will soon turn,'' said Eugenius, ''and we must kedge out into the channel, heave ho and smartly there, damn your butterfingers, boy! avast and hoist the topgallon, unfurl the futtockshrouds, man the mandible, jiggle your jissom now,'' and many other similar sounds which meant as much, or as little, as any of the Eddessan's theology to Peregrine and to Claud; and but little to Appledore, and that little long and all but lost in the mists of time. But, somehow, and perhaps owing to the beneficence of the Great Water Worm, an Emanation in whose existence Eugenius was certainly convinced, the morning found them sailing down the swelling surface of the buxom flood.

"Fortunate it was," said the Ophite, at length satisfied, "that I had already laden me my vessel for a voyage, and to be sure they will all back there believe that I did so with foreknowledge of their impending and intended raid. And glad am I that they will, for then they will suspect each other, ah hah hah hah," he laughed grimly. "Now, let me see. They will learn that I had said I intended to sail downstream, so they will think that I will think that they would think that I would instead sail *up*stream. Therefore they will *expect* me to sail downstream. Which I will anyway, for the new Caesar's writ runneth not past those waters which we have already passed. And, more to the point, perhaps, neither does that of the Bishop of the Fourth Ward, South, the fanatic.

Peregrine, perched on the prow with a fishing-line attached to his great toe, looked up. "The Bishop of the Third Ward, South?"

"No, no, boy, the Bishop of the *Fourth* Ward, South. The Bishop of the Third Ward, South, is a mere visionary, spending all his time at it. And the Bishop of the Fourth Ward, *North*, is a voluptuary, spending all his time at *it*. But the Bishop of the Fourth Ward, South, ah, there is one you have to watch out for: a gaunt ascetic of the worst gaunt ascetic type, with a long and boney nose ever eager to sniff out heresies as he calls them. Why! Twas not a month since that he interrupted the Divine Liturgy—so-called, but perforce I had to attend, else he'd have had my kidneys crucified before you could say Kyrie Eleison—to proclaim a hue and cry against the limner of the very synaxarion he had been chanting from; and for why? For that the limner in his illumination for the Sixth Sunday after Sex-

tuagesima had depicted Christ as wearing blue and gold
robes after the Resurrection instead of purple and gold
robes, for Christ should then having been wearing
purple, the mourning of princes, he being Prince of
Princes, and in mourning for himself—that is, to speak
more precisely his Divine nature should have been
shown as wearing mourning for his Human Nature,
however—and from this that fanatic, the Bishop of the
Fourth Ward, South, did deduce and adduce that the
limner was an heretic, "A Valentinian or worse, if
worse there be," he said—forasmuch as he did deny
that Jesus in any form died upon the Cross, but hinting
by means of his illuminated limnings that a phantom
took the place of Jesus and—

"But now I piddle upon the purple of the Bishop of
the Fourth Ward, South, and let him swim, an he
wishes now to seek out and confront me, ah hah hah,"
he laughed grimly. And he told in relishing tones of
what had once been done to an anti-Ophitical bishop in
the good old days gone by, omitting no torture however
slight. And then he shifted his helm in order to avoid
causing severe scandal to a fish-weir.

Peregrine gazed upon the master of the vessel, the
wool-merchant and arch-heresiarch, in no small wonder, as the man sat with the stick of the helm in his aft
armpit. For the moment, safety and the memory of
ancient revenges, as well as the clean fresh air of the
river, had brought a sparkle to his eyes. But the fur-
rowed skin around those eyes, the sagging cheeks, the
lines descending from eyes to cheekbones, from nose to
jowels, told of something different, something more
usual. And Peregrine wondered about him, and about
the other harried followers of equally strange sects and
occult cults, tired of the farce called the *Pax Romana*,
under which their hurried sacraments of bread and
milk, their offering of the Cup to serpents, may yet at

some future day obtain them a crown in paradise, but which were far likelier and more definitely to do so at the price of a red-hot-iron crown on earth.

Aloud, Peregrine said, musingly, "To think that only yesterday morning my friends and I narrowly escaped the press-gang, and—"

"The press-gang! Great Sacred Snakes! Do not mention the word, lest it come to pass. The *press-gang* was active yesterday, you say? This bodes no good."

This puzzled the young man. Surely, he suggested, since the writ of the Caesar in power of the river ran not hither—

"The writ of Caesar hath little or nothing to do with it!" declared Eugenius, with vehemence. "The Imperial Fleet hath a writ of its own, a will of its own, and a way of enforcing that will which belikes me not at all. For some years now, in fact, Romanus, Arch-Admiral of the Inland Fleet, has carefully been omitting the names of the local caesars from his orders, and whilst he claims he does it for simplicity's sake alone, it being too difficult to keep changing, and sometimes not being cognizant on water of everything which has taken place on land, still, I am not so sure. My life has not been such so as to render me other than suspicious. So, for all that he modestly claims that he is merely the servant of the Emperor, and goes on at a great rate about how the Throne is never vacant and the fleet serves the Throne, that is, the Empire in its entirety, rather than being limited to any one man . . still . . . still . . ."

And his mutters and mumbles died away, Peregrine took a deep breath of the riverine air, and gazed all about him with pleasure. Claud sat stock-still in dead center of the boat, and although he looked somewhat less expectant of semi-instant death by drowning, it was only somewhat so. Appledore had stripped down to the buff and had tied all his clothes to a line which he was towing behind by way of laundering, now and again giving it a jerk and a tumble, and now and then breaking into an old chanty in a cracked and off-key voice. And when Peregrine yelled and grabbed, first for his toes, and then for the line attached to it, it was Appledore who came running and brought the catch (a fine sterlet) aboard, deftly killed and cleaned it, and deftly set a caboose of coals to burning and busied himself with garlic and garum and parsley and salt and oil.

Peregrine, licking his fingers contentedly, watched the plump hills sliding by, the tilth and woodland, the vineyards and the meadows, green where the sun shone on it and blue where the clouds intruded between sun and shore. A smaller stream entered the main flow not far ahead, and on a small neck of land between the two unequal waters a townlet sat staunchly. Eugenius gestured to Peregrine.

"Now, carefully note and observe," he instructed him, "that the prow is pointed dead set between those two huge trees on yonder island, eh? Keep her so, till and until and unless I bid you otherwise," and with that he relinquished the tiller, and stood upon the half-lid of the squat water butt and shaded his eyes and gazed ashore. Peregrine stared at the prow and concentrated upon keeping it centered between the two trees until he almost felt his eyes crossing.

"I am unsure," Eugenius said, low-voiced. "I am uncertain. Yonder is Galicum, a prosperous enough wee port with an hundred looms, give or take a few; usually a good port to put into with wool and fells. But now . . . I am not persuaded . . . . It does look quiet . . . perhaps it looks too quiet . . . Well, in another moment I must make up my mind, or the current will not carry us there, howe'er so much I turn my tiller, and to beat upstream would— *Ah, woe!"*

And hard upon his lamentation, from out of nowhere that Peregrine could clearly observe, a long low vessel legged with many oars darted forth and raced forward across the water like a living thing starved for and intent on prey, its limbs flashing in the sunlight. Peregrine jumped up and then as swiftly sat down again, then took a swift look all about: but nowhere might he see any other vessel or destination or object which could have caused the Eddessan's alarm.

"Is that not a galley?" asked he. "And is it coming after us? And for what and for why? And what shall we do?"

In his ear, Appledore said, "It is not only a galley, it is a dromon, and if it is not the swiftest ship upon this stretch of water, 'twill do for that description."

And Eugenius, with a gesture, swept Peregrine from the tiller, and abruptly changed the course of his own slow sailing-barge: and at that time, a sound, faint but emphatic, came cracking over the water. But by the time it reached their eyes, the dromon had also changed course, and still it headed for them, and for them, (it seemed) alone.

"Jettison the cargo!" ordered Eugenius.

"He means, throw the bales overboard," Appledore translated. "Go, now! Move boys!"

Peregrine had more than once played some small and light role at shearing-time at home, and the smell of sheep-suint and sheep-sweat and sheep-oil had brought it back to his memory again. But in an instant more he learned that while a fleece is a light weight to toss, an hundred fleeces bounded and bonded into a bale are a less light weight indeed. Claud at that moment broke the spell which had held him fast, and, forgetful of previous fears, clambered down and took hold of the rough drugget which contained the pressed wools. With a heave and a strain and a drag, they got it to the side—and let it escape from their dragging fingers into the dappled wetness alongside and beneath; one brief moment they watched it sink, then dragged themselves away, and took the next; by the time they returned with the second, the first had bobbed to the surface. Appledore, unseen, instead of lending a hand, had seemingly given himself over to despair, and of him they could hear only a wailing chant.

Within a matter of moments Peregrine's hair, sweat-wet and -slicked, was obscuring his eyes, and he hoped that Claud could see where they were going; he tugged, he allowed himself to be tugged and dragged.

Once, indeed, the bale having slipped, he allowed himself a second to wipe his eyes clear, and saw the dromon lunging forward. Then he bent again to his task. The wailing chant went on and on and it seemed unendurable; he could hear the *bong-bong-bong* of the semantron, as the bailiff on the dromon relentlessly, remorselessly beat out the rhythm for the rowers. And he could hear the sharp, crisp, and—it seemed—cruel commands—although he could make nothing of the words themselves—which someone, presumably an officer, was issuing: and he could imagine that they referred to such things as he had heard and read of (far-off days, a million years behind, he and Austin small boys in some small and clean room in the palace precincts back in Sapodilla, and Appledore as tutor), grappling-hooks and the short swords used in close combat.

And then he heard something else, heard the officer's voice rising, going out of control, heard half a hundred voices suddenly drown the other out, heard alarm, heard fear, heard the tone of command regain control and, barely kept within control and high-pitched, issue another order, this one very rapid, broken off—heard a sound he had never in his life before heard, barely even imagined, like that of a hundred wagons crashing together (this, the best he was able to do, in that one flashing second, towards explaining what he heard to himself)—and the screams, and the screaming—

Where but a breathing-space before he had seen the dromon coursing down the stream and all the bales of wool bobbing before in its path, now he saw the stream studded with rocks, each the size of a bale of wool, saw the dromon at an impossible angle—what speed! with what speed must she have rushed to her destruction despite all attempts—hanging halfway in the air and halfway on its side, and oddest of all how some of the oars still rowed—men slipping into the water, men striving desperately not to slip, men bobbing in the water like bales of wool, though so oh much smaller—

Twisting and turning his head, Peregrine saw Eugenius desperately porting his helm, felt the barge respond, saw Appledore, was aware that the droning chant was suddenly stopped, saw the rocks once more change to bales of wool, saw the dromon slip down and under and under and— Saw Appledore's cheeks fill with breath, heard the strange sharp whistle; which long long later he was to identify as the sound of a wind-borne sea-bird in a certain Northern Sea, heard the sail, which had been luffing, suddenly fill with wind. Saw faces very near in the water. Saw one set of eyes take hold of his own, saw that one face mark his own face, knew that they would know each other's faces if they were to meet a century later at the farthest end of the Erythrian Sea, or farther . . .

Eugenius huddled at his helm, the wind rose high, the sailing-barge charged forward, the island and its two trees, the port of Calicum and its hundred looms fell, all fell, fell far behind.

The furrow followed free.

For a long, long time no one said anything. Then Appledore, in an abstracted manner, slowly drew from the water the line holding his garments, undid the knot, wrung them out, and began to put them on, breaking the silence with the low-voiced comment that they would dry on him. Eugenius seemed to come-to with a start.

"Nay, nay," he said. "For all that as a good Gnostic Christian I should abstain from all sorts of magic, yet under the circumstances I cannot find it in me to do other than to feel appreciative for your twain favor to me, that is, in changing the bales of wool into rocks to wreck that damned dromon, and then in raising a wind and thus enabling us to get far from the reach of any second dromon, or for that matter any other craft which might have been havening at Calicum . . . and, for *that* matter, of any of the ship's survivors who might have attempted to board us from the water . . .

"What I mean to say is: In the cubby there are clean clothes, some of which should certainly fit you, and all of which are dry."

Appledore emerged from the cubby not only with dry clothes, but with a rough chart of the river, which he had found below hanging from a peg. "Nimrunna," he said, "is next port below, I perceive."

Eugenius nodded thoughtfully. "Nimrunna is next, and let us hope Nimrunna is more peacefully inclined to us than Calicum, for the channel of the river thereabouts is such that we must swing in so close to shore there that, were the city captured by a mutiny of schoolboys, they might sweep our decks with apples.

"However, if all goes well, we may perhaps be able to pick up a cargo there, as the All-Seeing Serpent knows where our original cargo now lies. And if no cargo, then I would load ballast, even if water ballast, for we now are so light we ride high—all very well in these narrows and shoals—but below Nimrunna commence the broads, currents are tricky, and I would not wish to depend upon further magic, should we be troubled.''

"Nor I," said Appledore, rather weakly.

But Polonius, the Prefect of the Port, greeted Eugenius as an old acquaintance. Howbeit, he expressed disappointment. "Why I had thought you would bring us some fine fells," he said, "for to make those sheepskin coats which justly fame our name, as well as many bales of prime wool for our well-known spinning and dyeing establishments. Strangers," he said, addressing Peregrine, Appledore, and Claud, "you may or may not have heard of Nimrunna before, away back in wherever you hail from, but you will hear of us wherever you may go from now on, yessirs, Nimrunna is a thriving place, Nimrunna is up-and-coming. Nimrunna eschews not only the indolence of paganism and the unworldliness of heresy, but the feverish yet unproductive excitement of fanaticism as well. And what's the consequence? Why, the consequence is that we here in Nimrunna are spreading our city limits and our city's products far and wide. A mere decade ago Nimrunna was little more than a place to take on water and pay tolls, so small that it had only a handful of citizens, not more than a hundred, with only three bishops, thirty churches, and half-a-dozen whorehouses; think of that!

"Whereas, thanks to industry and immigration and the reign of that most benign and intelligent of Caesars, Augustus XXV, who often laughingly refers to himself as Stingy Gus, we here in Nimrunna can now boast of fifteen sawmills, ten boatyards, thirty kilns producing the widest range of pottery products conceivable, from penny oil lamps to vintage-season amphorae; we have two score smithies, of which eleven provide prime service for horse and mule alike, the other nine specializing in ox-forgework, thirteen thread mills, four-and-forty oil-presses, thirty dye-works, six sausage-, ham-, and bacon-smokehouses, five fullers' yards, and what good is it all if no cargo comes in? If you don't sell you can't buy, and all I observe aboard are three strangers, mighty welcome of course, but not for sale are they, ho ho ho, but no wool, confound it—only the smell!''

And he gave a dry chuckle and a jovial wheeze, but there was that in his aspect which bespoke one who missed his tolls, his excises, fees, ad valorems, customs duties, and in particular his traditional perquisites; and rather hungrily he eyed the saddlebags, all that remained of what had come forth out of Sapodilla.

"Now, now," cautioned Eugenius, "you know that you are not to levy upon personal gear which has travelled fewer than five ports along the river; and moreover, this fine young stripling is blood-kin to an Allied King and hence free of all and any imposts, and the other two are, respectively, his personal physician and tutor, and his body-servant.''

The prefect raised his hands and bowed and looked suitably impressed . . . but still his eyes roved round and darted to and from the saddlebags . . . and so Peregrine said, "Are you not by virtue of your post and office authorized to make payments on behalf of the Imperial Bursary to those having the appropriate parchment scrip?''

At the mention of the words, *make payment*, the prefect's eyes grew large and he began to shake his head, and by the time Peregrine had finished the prefect's eyes were very large indeed and his head almost wobbled with the vigor with which he hastened to deny the very possibility and indeed the very propriety of his being asked to pay, rather than to collect.

"Ah, no no no and no!" he declared. "Of course you are a stranger and so you would not be aware that— It is quite out of the question for— The office of the prefect and that of the bursar are two entirely separate and distinct func- func- functions, functions distinct and, or, that is," and finally he paused and collected the words for the essential phrase so dearly beloved to civil servants in all times and in all climes: *"That is not my department!"*

Then, with some degree of haste, he invited the newcomers to attend services at any of the city's seventy-five churches, all quite clear of any taint of heresy; as well as those provided by the ninety-nine brothels, all of which were government-inspected and fully-licensed. Then he bowed and withdrew.

Claud spoke first. "Ninety-nine," he said, awed.

Peregrine snorted. "Just tell them who you are," he suggested, "and show them what you've got."

The sarcasm passed over Claud's head. "No," he said, "that wouldn't work. You've got to pay them money."

"Surely you can think of something else?"

Claud digested this, and came to a reluctant conclusion. "You mean," he said, "that we haven't got any more money?"

"I mean that we haven't got any more money, is what I mean."

Claud got briskly to his feet. "Boy!" he called, to a dock-side lounger old enough to have been his father. "Which way is the Imperial Bursary?"

It was quite a long way. "I miss my mule," said Claud.

Appledore grunted. "When had you ever been favored with a mule before?" he asked. *"I* miss my jackass, the Child of Abraxas. Your mule were merely one which happened to be issued to you by the stable-thralls as part of Peregrine's entitles, but the ass-Child of Abraxas I more-or-less made myself from the primal elements.''

''You made him out of a second-hand hide and a bag of bones which were Queen Calpurnia's idea of a joke, and by means of the foulest magic a real pagan would be ashamed to use, I bet,'' countered Claud.

Appledore said, somewhat smugly, ''If life hands you a lemon, make lemonade.''

The streets of Nimrunna were impeccably clean, which was rather strange, and totally devoid of loungers, which was stranger still. And although people were seen going into the churches and cathedrals, and coming out of them, none of them were gathered outside discussing divine theology or sacred metaphysics or, indeed, anything else. Everyone bustled, and everyone seemed to be carrying something, either a bulk object such as a board or a brick, or a string-bag full of merchandise, or a box of tools, or at least a single tool. One such, who gave them a sidelong look as he passed, was carrying an axe; and him Peregrine hailed.

''Are you a woodsman, sir?'' he asked.

The man snorted. ''Why don't you ask me if I'm a cameleopard while you're at it? No, of course I'm no woodsman, I was educated a rhetorician, but that game's washed up now.''

''Why then do you carry an axe?''

''Because if I was carrying a book of rhetoric, Stingy Gus would have me shackled in a second as being a non-productive element; and toting smashed rock in a gravel quarry would be the death of me. Of course he knows very well that I barely know one end of this vile implement from another, but I am obliged to pay trade-tax as a woodsman, and I *do* pay trade-tax as a woodsman, you can bet your foreskin. Besides, it looks well.''

"What, my foreskin?"

"Greek fire upon you, boy! The axe, the axe!"

And with a scowl, he drew apart from them and rebuffed further efforts to draw him into conversation. However, on hearing and reflecting, Claud showed an unexpected and in fact a previously unsuspected desire to help carry the saddle-bags, whilst Appledore armed himself with a sheet of clean papyrus and a reed pen behind his ear. "I hope they'll take me for a public scribe," he explained, "but I hope they won't take me so much for a public-scribe so as to demand evidence that I have paid trade-tax for being a public scribe."

The Imperial Bursary was quite a surprise in more ways than one. "This *is* the Imperial Bursary . . . *is* it?" asked Peregrine.

"Certainly it is," said the man behind the small and heavily-grated window. "Why should you doubt it?" He was tall and lean and had close-cropped hair and close-cropped beard and long, lean jaws. "State your business."

But Peregrine was not quite ready yet to state his business. "I wasn't exactly *doubt*ing it," he explained. "Only for a moment I thought it looked like a church, I mean, not an old church, formerly the temple of an abomination, but one of the new and modern-type churches, with thick walls and little windows, you see."

"Certainly I see. It *is* a church, to be precise it is the Church of Saint Epaminondas of Epididymus, but it is also the Imperial Bursary, and is located here precisely because of the thickness of the walls and the littleness of the windows. Divine Liturgy is celebrated here on each Saint's Day at high noon . . . each Saint Epaminondas Day, I mean, in order to maintain the franchise. Formerly the Dole for Aged, Indigent, and Cripples was distributed here, but by the wisdom of the

August Caesar, Augustus XXV, that has been discontinued as leading to the encouragement of unproductive elements; however, foundling children are still received here between seven and twelve every evening; state your business.''

Peregrine chuckled.

''Very little seems to get past Stingy Gus,'' he said.

''Very little does,'' said the lean-jawed man, ''and do you know why?''

Peregrine chuckled again. ''No. Why?''

''Because *I* am Stingy Gus. *State your business.*''

\*   \*   \*   \*

The Imperial Bursary offered to redeem Peregrine's scrip, but only at an enormous discount; attempts to move Augustus XXV to be more generous by appealing to the case of *Theme of Bithynia vs. Estate of the Protopresbyter of Cyrenaica* proved total failures.

''Well,'' said Appledore, ''as he himself said, in fact, as the commissary-major said, you can always appeal. Meanwhile, you continue to retain scrip supposedly for the full value of the sequestered items at current prices; and you might try seeing what that will purchase at a butchery or bakery.''

''Or a brothelry,'' suggested Claud.

''You have a singularly narrow mind.''

''What I have is a singularly heavy prong.''

They were offered, after considerable very dubious perusal of the parchmentry, five loaves of bread apiece every day for fifty-five days; and some similar bargain in lambs livers, goats' melts, and rabbit tongues. They looked at each other, first with despair, then with a wild surmise, and, by unspoken consent, found their way to another district, where the lights were brighter, or, at least, redder.

"My family used to own one of the biggest latifundia in East Nubia," the matron Eudoxia explained to Peregrine, as she poured wine in her best painted chamber. Appledore was elsewhere, discussing philosophy with one of Eudoxia's associates who had (she had assured him) spent a lot of time minding the stoa; and Claud was in another compartment yet, taking the weight off his prong with the coöperation of a stalwart young woman who specialized in such cases. "I'm telling you all this because I can see that you're not just an ordinary client, but one used to the better things in life." She looked at him from beneath her painted eyelashes.

"As you are yourself," he said, taking the cup.

The matron Eudoxia heaved a deep sigh, an act which did extraordinary things to her rather extraordinary bosom. "Oh, my pappa daddy would just turn over in his sarcophagus if he were to see some of the foul fates which have befallen me," she said, "before I was enabled by a kindly providence to set up this establishment for wine-tasting and conversation. Although just how I am to keep it all together, what with the priests and the bishops calling me a second Hypatia, not to speak of the *taxes*, O my Saints and Martyrs! is more than I can say. Still, I never lose hope, if good fortune is predestined for one, not all the priests and bishops and taxes in the world can prevent it, that's what I believe. That's what I used to tell this girl Theodora, we used to feed the bears together back in Byzantium, 'Keep your chin up, Theo, and encourage the right kind of client, and your luck is bound to change, a lovely girl like you with a good head on her shoulders,' I used to say. And see what happened? She married a Caesar's nephew.

"Far be it from me to knock the government, after all, the Central Roman Empire is the land of opportun-

ity, everybody knows that, and I'd be the last to be-
grudge contributing my just share to keeping those
awful barbarians at bay—why, I used to know a girl, a
really lovely person, and it was her fate to be captured
by a Hun horde, and then to be re-captured by a cohort
of Imperial troops: what *she* told *me!*

"But, now, as to this scrip, and all that," said the
matron Eudoxia, getting down to business, "I ap-
preciate your being frank with me, I know what it is not
to have ready cash and what you might call liquid
assets, and it's true that I do have a lot of contacts with
high-placed people, which is always a help. Of course
we are all good Christians nowadays ["Of course,"
said Peregrine, looking deep into his wine-cup.], and
there is after all *noth*ing like a good theological rag-
chew about such eternal verities as, *is* the Son made out
of nothing, or is the Son made out of something, and if
so, what *kind* of something . . . or, for that matter, I
guess, what kind of nothing? These things are
im*por*tant!"

However, important as they were, Eudoxia would,
she admitted, be the first to admit that one cannot spend
all of one's good times discussing theology. One must
spend some of one's good time at wine-tasting and
conversation as well— "But some of these little pesky
priests and badmouthing bishops, I mean, *I* know what
saintly priests and bishops are *like!* They don't make
them, they just don't *make* them, the way they used to
make them down in East Nubia; why the desert was just
*crawl*ing with saints when I was a girl, you didn't dast
throw a *stick* for fear of hitting an anchorite or a ceno-
bite or an heremite, and every ruined portico, which
formerly the pillars supported the portico of a temple of
an abomination, every *pillar* had a preacher living on
the top of it— But hereabouts and nowadays, the priests
and bishops, as they call themselves," and here she

gave a scornful snortle, *"I* know all about *them!* Why, would you believe it, some of them eat *meat?* Some of them *bathe?* Some of them are even," and she leaned forward to import an horrid confidence in an horrified and low-voiced tone, "some of them are even *married!"*

"No!"

"Yes! You call that being a priest or a bishop? How can he mortify his flesh properly if he gets laid every night in his own bed? You call *that* mortifying the flesh? Huh! So! *Let* them denounce me. *Let* them threaten to tear me to pieces with sharpened oyster-shells. It's a funny thing about me, I have to tell the truth, let the chips fall where they may, and I am totally unable to dissimulate, so let them threaten to stone me, as if I was afeared of them, why—"

At that very moment there was a sound of shouting in the street and a rattle of stones fell against the walls, and Eudoxia, shrieking in terror, flung herself upon Peregrine, spilling his wine.

"Tear her to pieces with sharpened oyster-shells!" a voice cried, one seeming not entirely devoid of clerical intonations. "Remission of 57,000 aeons in Purgatory for he who tears off the first piece!"

The mob growled. And another voice declaimed, "Stone her! Stone the foreign slut Eudoxia, the doxy!"

"All East Nubians are Monophysites, if not worse, if worse there be!"

"Stone her!"

Screams and cries of alarm and terror began to resound from the other chambers of Eudoxia's establishment for wine-tasting and conversation. From the street came an hysterical shriek of, "Flay the undoubtedly heretical denier of perfectly lawful clerical incelibacy, and thus the enemy of wholesome family life": this, in a female voice.

And, "Burn her alive after tearing her to pieces with sharpened oyster-shells, for taking the bread out of the mouths of native-born and doctrinally honest prostitutes!" shouted another woman.

Eudoxia hissed her scorn. "Oh, that bitch, Zoe, she has the ugliest girls in town at her house, she's always hated me— Save me! Save me! What do I pay trade-taxes for?"

This consideration had evidently entered the mind of at least one other person, for in a sudden lull in the shouting and tumult of the mob, and while the other denizens of the house came running in, in sundry states of disarray, followed by Claud and Appledore, a voice outside was heard—

"Get home, now! Get on about your business! Return to your requisite and productive occupations, and terminate this unlawful assembly, or I'll call the cohorts!"

The silence was short-lived. "Down with Stingy Gus!" someone shouted. And, "Let's raid and burn the Bursary!" shouted someone else. The voice of Stingy Gus continued to be heard, and was now heard calling for the cohorts, but in rapidly diminishing tone, as though coming from someone engaged in quickly quitting the scene.

"*Deposed is Augustus the XXV, protector of Monophysitism!*"

"*Down with the crypto-Donatist, Augustus the Penurious!*"

"*Let's burn all the tax-bills and proclaim a generous and leisure-loving Caesar!*"

"*And one whose anti-Monophysitism is beyond question!*"

"*Redeem from mammon the Church of Saint Epaminondas of Epididymus!*"

Peregrine, meanwhile, had led both staff and patronage of Eudoxia's establishment into the rear atrium, each of whom, or each pair of whom, he had bidden by gestures to carry along a bench. Out front the unity of the mob was being threatened by a sudden revival of the question of the Procession of the Third Person of the Trinity. Peregrine began to pile the benches on top of one another, and against the wall.

"Ask Bishop Buffo, here— It's his ward, ain't it? Ask him, go on, ask him, ask him don't the Holy Spirit proceed from the—" And another and even louder voice, perhaps anticipating and not relishing Bishop Buffo's reply, declared that that prelate would eat an unspeakable substance with a rusty spoon.

Peregrine clambered up to the top of the wall, having prudently thrown several cloaks' thickness over the broken glass embedded there, and beckoned for Claud and Appledore to hand him up more benches. And in another several seconds, Eudoxia and her ladies had climbed up, climbed over, and climbed down into the dimness on the other side.

\* \* \* \*

The other streets had been drained of traffic by the activity, and there was almost no one about in port when the fugitives came galloping down upon the docks. A figure jerked up from slumber on the deck of a vessel moored to the quay, and began to intone, "Passage now available for all downstream ports, with connections for the Danube and the Euxine Sea! Sailing-barge *Homoiousios* now loading! New, low prices, and— Oh. It's you. And you. And you, too. Also— But who are *you?*"

"Religious refugees," said Peregrine, briefly. "Cast off!"

"Fares payable strictly in advance," said Eugenius.

And he declined to consider offers to take it out in trade. However, as the young lady explained, who had been assisting Claud, reasons of convenience oft-times obliged her to remove her clothes, but reasons of prudence forbade her from ever removing her savings. Eugenius accepted two bracelets and an ear-bauble from her in return for deck-passage, and was in process of assessing the tariff for the matron Eudoxia and her other associates in the wine-tasting and conversation trade, when Peregrine interrupted.

"These details can wait, wool-master," he urged. "There are great civil disturbances disturbing the peace of Nimrunna, and the populace is making mighty use of the word heresy, wherefore—"

The Eddessan, with a whoop, hiked up the skirts of his robe, and scuttled down the deck betimes to set in the rudder, calling over his shoulder, "Cast off, there, boy! Cast off—O Sweet Suffering Serpent, against Whom Ialdabaoth did raise up the heel of man!" But the mooring lines had tightened more than Peregrine's 'prentice-boy hands could quickly loosen, and the ship's owner moaned with fear, "O Sweet Prunicos Her pudenda! Hasten, hasten, lad!—else we be but butchers' meat, for do I not now hear the approach of the Caesar himself, accompanied by at least one cohort?"

Not only did they hear him, they almost immediately saw him, and would have seen him sooner, had not the Caesar himself, previously and penuriously ordered two out of every three lamps on the quays to be extinguished after the tenth hour. He came into sight at a rapid pace, slapping the sides of an enormous and enormously laden dray-horse, and behind him could be heard at least one cohort, which might have made a more rapid progress, did they not pause every few paces to smite the stone paving with the butt-ends of their spears and chant, *"Christ conquers!"* Discipline, however, was discipline.

"Passage! Passage!" shouted Stingy Gus, on perceiving the vessel about to shove off.

Eugenius at once ceased his moans, crisply ordering, "All hands fall to and load passenger's baggage, look lively there, avast!" The bags were exceedingly heavy, and they clinked. "That will be five bezants for Your Highness's passage, and five bezants apiece per bag, payable in advance," said Eugenius.

The long jaws of the Caesar clamped shut, to unclamp immediately and say, "Extortionate! Cite me a soother sum, else I shall strive to reach an accommodation with the yonder troops."

"They don't call you 'Stingy Gus' for nothing, Stingy Gus. Well, well, I shall abate one bezant per bag, subject, however, to demurrage, bottomry, flotsam, jetsam, perils of other princes and potentates, mutiny of the master, mates, or men, as well as ambush, adumbration, hypothecation, usurpation, pilot charges in shoal waters—the vessel now being heavy-laden with your gear—and all other perils of the seas, the shallows, and the inland waters; got that line loose, lad? Drop her then and jump, else swim."

Stingy Gus looked longingly from baggage to shore, then, a spear whistling through the air and thudding into the deck not an hand's span away from him, he yelped, and dove into the cubby-hold for cover. And the vessel swung into the stream and into the darkness.

\* \* \* \*

The deck was wet with cold dew when Peregrine, who had the dog-watch, awoke and shuffled forward, rubbing his eyes and scratching his crotch; and relieved himself at the stern. "You can get some sleep now," he said to Eugenius.

The Eddessan's grunt was faint, but scornful. "Why, you have spent all of a day on this river, and you think to be able to pilot at night? Though you were my own son, and cradled on this current from the day of thy chrismation, I'd not trust the vessel to thy sole charge at night. Nay, nay, sit here beside me and take the tiller so that I may rest my arm; then by and by we come to a safe cove for anchor: *then* I will try for sleep, leaving you to stand guard."

Peregrine took the tiller and sat down. He laughed, listening to the snores of the others, in quantity and volume almost beyond belief. A faint glow came from the setting moon, casting long and thick, deep shadows from the trees and hills. The cool air was clean, and the rank, musty smell of wool and sheepskin was somewhat fainter now. Something stirred in his mind, and he took the occasion to speak of it.

"Let me cite you a saying, Master," he said. "May I—?"

"Cite away, sonny."

" 'Burn the baleful signs indited on boards of beechwood—' what does that signify to you?"

Some small sound of stirring night-life from the shore distracted the both of them for a moment; then the Eddessan said, thoughtfully, "Why . . . besides the fact of its author having a taste for alliteration . . . that the saying had its source either in or not far from some place where beech-trees grow. I'd not look for that source in, say, Syrene, or Babylon . . . And what does it signify to *you,* my cockerel?"

Peregrine considered if he should or not disclose to the Eddessan what Mother Boadicea had reded for him from the Sibylline Book. How well did he know him, could trust him? His answer came equally slow. "Why . . . it is in some way connected with my fate and future . . ."

"And are you contented with your fate? Do you fear your future, with these baleful boards in it?"

"I am content enough, I wanted to see more of the world, and I am seeing more of it. And I wanted to have interesting adventures, and I am having them. No . . . no . . . I don't fear my future, though naturally I have some concern about it. I wonder about my own place, now, in the world. I didn't use to wonder about it, in my native land my place, though subordinate and limited, was both certain and agreeable. Each day was very like another. No day out in the wider world has, so far, been any very much like another."

The Eddessan rather gently placed his hand on Peregrine's wrist, and turned the tiller to port, the boat in turn turning to starboard. Water burbled quietly off a half-sunken log. Then he set her back on her previous course. "I am older than you by almost two generations," he said. "I have travelled far. Of my joys and of my sorrows I do not now speak. Days differ, as people differ, face from face and nature from nature. But each body has the same set of bones as each other body. And so has each day. We lie us down, we rise us up, we eat and drink and stoop to stool. The day in which we do these simple services may not seem to be a particularly good one, but let a day come which prevents us from doing any of those, and we may rightfully look back upon a day which did not, and say, 'Ah . . . *That* was a good day, yes! That day I was and did well!' "

Peregrine sighed and shifted and cleared his gullet, the way young people do when in receipt of good counsel. "Yes, yes, and so . . . But I am younger than you, Master, by almost two generations, and I have not travelled far. And I do hope that the time is not yet come for me when I can say of a good day only that I lied me down, I rose me up, I ate and I drank and I stooped to stool. This would be a good day for a poor man's dog, sir, but 'tis not yet to be accounted in its bare bones as a good day for Peregrine the son of Paladrine; no, sir."

Eugenius chuckled softly. Then he half-arose and he peered full into the darkness, cupping his ear. "Was that not the belling of a full-grown stag? And are those not three small eddies, one after the other? And is this not the quiet cove I am seeking of? Pere-boy, crouch by the jib and put your arm up, but limberly, with line in that hand—if a tree-limb touch it by my count of three, toss the line over the limb, and so make fast this barge."

It came about just as he predicted. Peregrine turned to see the other lifting the pane of horn in the ship's lamp and opening his lips to blow the wan flame out. "Master, has a name been set to this place?" he asked.

Eugenius shook out a sheep's pelt which had escaped the general exodus of the fleeces, and spread it under the bench. "Aye. Tis called the Upper Cove on Tufa Island . . . And now," he said, lowering himself rather stiffly, and drawing his cloak around him, "now I shall compose my limbs for sleep and my thoughts upon the Sacred Serpent, particularly in its present manifestation as this river, which has twice afforded us escape: and you may keep watch and ward."

Gradually, his eyes growing more accustomed to the darkness, though the lamp was out and the moon had set, Peregrine could or thought he could see better; and he saw a line of something light-colored, which he took for a beach of sorts: and he thought that it might be pleasant to go for a swim when it was light enough. Already he missed the comforts of a daily bath. Venus burned bright and great and cast her own shadows, and he bethought him of the temple in her name in Sapodilla Town, with its good marble copy of a good Grecian statue, slender and white: though the peasantry pre-ferred to worship her in a cave in the forest in the form of a squat, dark stone, rudely carved in the semblance of a female with enormous breasts and enormous belly and enormous buttocks, under the fond, familiar title of *Big Mamma;* disdaining all specious fashion and intent upon fundamentals only.

He thought of his first visit to that cave in company of his brother Austin, and with that his thoughts began to stray into wonderment as to where this older and so well-beloved brother might have gone to, and to what the chances of their being together again might be. And then he felt a hand take his ankle and even while the hairs rose upon his flesh and one hand groped for a weapon and his lips opened and closed, he heard the voice of Eugenius saying, "Summon the next watch."

He stuck his toes into Claud's ribs, who muttered, "C'mere, honey . . . Hey? . . . Honey? . . . Oh. *You. Cacadaemon!*"

Despite Claud's strenuous activities in the establishment of Matron Eudoxia, he had still (Peregrine observed) or again, a singularly heavy prong. Himself rolling up in the warmed blanket, he began to think of the events of the day until, soon enough, the night claimed him for her own.

He awoke, as he had fallen asleep, to the sound of several battery of snores. Claud was in process of waking Appledore, and neither was disposed to converse, the one not yet fully apart from slumber and the other eager to return to it. Augustus the Penurious lay sprawled in what would have seemed the full throes of unheeding sleep, had Peregrine not noticed that at least some part of the man's long body and long limbs was in contact with his baggage. And Eugenius the Eddessan, though dawn was breaking, puffed softly in and out between his cloak and his sheepskin.

There seemed no immediate prospect of any sudden burst of activity and departure, so Peregrine did no more than poke up the caboose for an ember and set a few charcoals upon it so that there might be fire enough when needed; then he stripped himself bare and slid by rope's aid down the side of the ship, noiselessly, into the cold, clean water. He was no great swimmer, the few ponds and one lake of his native state not producing any such, but he made his way well enough, and silently enough, by the stroke they called "frog-paddle." At first he thought to make directly for the beach, but there was still grey and mist all about, and no great pleasure to be had in shivering on the sands. Instead, he tackled the current, which was somewhat strong on this side of the Island, at least, with intent to drift back towards the beach on it when the day had had a chance to warm; and also he took care to keep within sound or sight of the boat, in case. Aside from this he was as mindless as any water-creature, and now he sported on the surface of the waves and now he bobbed his feet along the softy bottom and now and then he submerged and swam between the two. He had just surfaced and was about to snort and bubble when the illusion of a voice said what seemed to sound in his water-clogged ears as, "The Great White Christ . . ."

Appledore had followed him and was babbling again, was his second thought: but then both a quick look round and some inrush of common sense assured him that Appledore had done and was doing nothing of the sort. A faint touch of heat fanned his face, and he thought he saw the air shimmering over a point of land and thicket very near and close to him. A water bird regarded him with indifference, as he let himself go adrift, fetching up in the lee of the point where he catched hold of a trailing branch and held himself in place: and all of this so quickly enough that he heard as

it were an echo repeating, "The Great White Christ
. . ."

*Perhaps some Varangians have made their over-
night camp here on route between Byzantium which
they call* Micklegarth *and their own far northern land*,
he thought to himself, recalling Appledore's comment
that this phrase was much in the use of those Northmen
who came south to 'list in the Imperial Guard. But, had
he understood Appledore aright, the words could only
have been used reverently by the Norse and Rus; and if
he could be sure of anything so unexpected it was that
the voice which had just now twice repeated the phrase
had done so with anything but reverence. And now a
second voice with samely tone began to speak, and
Peregrine sank a little deeper into the water till the
wavelets lapped upon his lips, so strong was the hate he
heard.

"Aye, always and always that Pallid Twin, the
White Christ, extends his sway, his followers striving
always and always to obliterate the very name and fame
of the Other. But even they dare never to remove the
words which give their false faith the lie," and here the
two voices joined in a deep and reverent recitation of
the words, *"Black am I but beautiful. . . ."*

Short was the silence. Then the second voice said,
"Take the red knife and cut red bread."

It was not till Peregrine had surfaced again and was
swimming as fast for the *Homoiousios* as he could
without making, unchampion swimmer that he was,
great sound and fury; that he began to think instead of
merely to act and to react, and he realized that he had
absolutely no memory of having submerged and taken
off from that point of land. He saw Eugenius scanning
the river as he came up, and he saw the Eddessan's face
change from concern into relief and then almost at once

into vexation; Peregrine heaved himself up from the water to put a finger to his lip and to make a gesture of alarm. The Eddessan stayed silent, but he moved close to the massive over-hanging limb whereon the vessel was moored, and from there he bent to help haul up Peregrine, bare and goose-prickly, and in this was assisted by Appledore, who had just come aft.

"Are they *there?*" Eugenius whispered.

Peregrine half-knelt, half-crouched, his wet and dripping hair leaching forward into a peak. Then he raised his head and said, softly and haltingly, that the "they" whom he had observed were not any Imperial officers nor any officials nor followers of any Imperial church, and, "As to whether they are truly members of any church at all, I cannot say, being not even an heretic myself, but, Appledore: Do you remember that one night when you—of which you said you hoped that we need never speak of it again between us—?"

Appledore nodded, then winced, then shrugged. "If need, then need. I have not after all sworn by the length of yon cable-tow to keep silence, nor to hele, conceal, and never reveal— Speak up, Per!

"But not too much up," he added, nervously.

Peregrine spoke but few words. Appledore and Eugenius exchanged swift glances. "If the red knife does be cutting red bread hereabouts," said the Eddessan, "it is exactly time to embark, and not a moment after time." Once more the barge left a mooring in haste enough. And there was no explanatory conversation. Peregrine thoughtfully dried his hair and donned his breech-clout. The day looked to be warm, and he felt a chill in his flesh and in his limbs and thought he might gratefully receive some sun.

Wine was poured into a basin and put on the brazier to mull, and, as though the fragrance of its fumes sent out a sort of olfactory signal, suddenly people began to get up. Matron Eudoxia was first, and she seemed to think, from a one or two or more looks and glances and sights, and sighs, that the supple-limbed form of Peregrine might prove perhaps a certain compensation for the loss of her franchise in the wine-tasting and conversation business back in Nimrunna; and after her came the other ladies, whom she greeted with a perhaps maternal and perhaps sororital concern, as:

"*Good* morning, Pulchrituda, if you are well, I am well, and it is well."

"Yes, Matron."

"*Good* morning, Philoxenia, if you are well, I am well, and it is well."

"Yes, Matron."

"*Good* morning, Pulchrituda, if you are well, I am well, and it is well—it *is?*—say—didn't I just see you and greet you coming up from down there just a minute ago?"

"No, Matron."

"But I say, yes."

"Say what you like, then."

The Matron Eudoxia put her hands on her hips, a gesture which gave her a stance not unlike that of a heavy-weight wrestler getting ready to grapple an opponent in the Hippodrome. "Listen, don't you talk to me like *that*, you nasty little chippy! Why, what were you when I got you but a bedraggled little slut working the booths in every tenth-rate crib in town?"

Pulchrituda slumped into a deceptive crouch, but kept her hands free, and one of them plucked a bodkin from her girdle. "Listen," she said, "you weren't so much yourself not too long ago from what I hear, and leave us not have any more of that catshit about your pappa daddy and biggest latifundia in West Suavia, either, see?"

Eudoxia screamed like a wounded peacock, seized the girl's wrist and twisted it so that the bodkin fell to the deck, then heaved the recalcitrant young woman over her shoulder; which shoulder the recalcitrant young woman took the opportunity to sink her teeth into, drawing another scream, and blood.

"First falernian for Pulchrituda," said Appledore, continuing, in the impartially judicial tones of a referee. "Pulchrituda is down and Eudoxia has her by the arms, but Pulchrituda by a very deft little feet-work has Eudoxia on her side and is giving her the old I-II-III in the ribs and now Eudoxia has Pulchrituda by the right knee and Pulchrituda goes down again, but Eudoxia isn't holding her, no citizens and senators, because Pulchrituda seems to be part snake and part wild-cat, and O lares and penates! look at her plucking out Eudoxia's hair by the handful, but now Pulchrituda is down again, she is *down!* and this time it seems that Eudoxia is going to fracture all of Pulchrituda's pretty little limbs, what a shame, but all's fair in the Games, citizens and senators: So what's your decision, O Senate and the People of Rome? Are the thumbs going to be down, too? Or are they going to be up? —up?—up—"

"Up yours, Grandpa!" said Philoxenia, with an infidel pagan oath which more than matched his, and with that she seized up the fallen bodkin and jabbed it into Eudoxia's left rump, shouting, "You let go of my chummy, you corn-fed sow!" Appledore at this perhaps felt that things had gotten a little out-of-hand—an opinion also held by one of the passengers who was moaning how unproductive the whole scene was— "They could at least turn it into an orgy and charge admission," he pointed out—Appledore grabbed up the bucket of river-water which had been hauled aboard to dilute the hot breakfast wine, and doused the contestants all, impartially.

"Oh dear," a soft, female voice said, "I am afraid that this is all *my* fault. You see, my name is also Pulchrituda, and so naturally I responded when greeted, and so . . . Oh dear. Oh, dear ladies, will you, can you forgive me?" And while most of the folk present looked on in simple confusion, Peregrine observed, rapidly, two things; firstly, that the last speaker did bear a definite resemblance to the other female of the same name; and, secondly, that she was none other than the somewhat reluctant companion of Mother Boadicea.

The Captain of the Sailing-barge *Homoiousios*, however, observed a thirdly, "*You* listed on my passenger-roster!" he exclaimed. "*You* haven't paid any fare! *You are a stowaway, woman!*"

Sister Pulchrituda hung her comely head.

Matron Eudoxia, however, had other thoughts.

"Forgive you, huh? Sure, I'll forgive you. *After* I finish turning you into catsmeat for what you made me do to my sweet and actually unoffending little kiddy, here—" And she heaved herself half-way to her feet, with a sullen set to her jaw.

Peregrine hastily stepped forward. "Matron, allow me to introduce you to a former acquaintance of mine," he said, and Eudoxia, still half-way to her feet, paused and allowed her eyes to wander from his face to his breech-clout and back again and he went on to say, "Matron Eudoxia, may I present to you Sister Pulchrituda, one of the only three authentic and intact Vestal Virgins. Sister Pulchrituda, Matron Eudoxia. —I hope," he said, earnestly, "that mere differences in religious preferences will not prevent you from becoming fast friends."

Eudoxia took one last and lingering look at his breech-clout, and rose rapidly to her feet, wiping her hands on her hips. "Why, perish the absolute thought!" she urged. "One of the only three authentic and intact Vestal whats?"

"Virgins," said Peregrine. "Sworn to chastity and poverty, you know," he added.

"Well, don't you worry about *poverty!*" said the matron in hearty and can-I-believe-my-*ears* tones. "Honey, you and I are going to be very *good* friends in-*deed*. Poverty, huh? Why, honey, don't you know that you're sitting on a fortune?"

Penurious Augustus, who had been looking and listening, and, towards the last, nodding very, very slowly, now suddenly looked up. His jaws fell, he shouted, fell upon his bags and hugged them as though they were imperiled and dearly-beloved children. "O my bezants and my solidi!" he gasped. "You damned bargee, look where you've led us! Get us out of here at once, at *once*, do you hear?—or else restore my fare to me immediately—"

"Yes," said Peregrine, following his eyes, "or we will all need it to pay some other fares to Charon."

For Eugenius of Eddessa, intent, first upon the fight and then upon the introductions, had allowed his barge to sink her nose into a sand-bar—hastily he let out all the reefs in his sails—hastily did Appledore shrilly whistle for to raise a wind—other shrill whistles and shrill whoops and bloodcurdling screams drowned out the philosopher's whistle—for between the sandbar and the shore was shallow, and the waters of the shallows were now being beaten into froth by the hooves of a multitude of horses—and Eudoxia moaned, "There goes the biggest goddamned fee any whorehouse ever had a chance to earn—'intact' did he say? Well, not for long, honey. Not for long . . ."

Squatty, bent to the backs of their wild little horses, screaming and whistling and whooping and hooting and waving their infamous spiked flails, the riders in the shallows came down incredibly fast upon the vessel. Claud grabbed Philoxena and flung her over his shoulder and leaped the aft rail, as she screamed vigorously, ''The Huns! O Holy Martyred Protopresbyters of Paphlagonia! *The Huns!* . . . .''

Eudoxia, once again, flung her arms around Peregrine, imploring him to save her, save her, save her, save her—

This time, however, it was level daylight and there were no concealing walls with unfrequented streets behind them. He patted her on her ample back, saying, ''There, there,'' and then to the aghast Eugenius he said, wryly, ''Well, today we may go to stool without stooping.''

And the hordes of the Huns raced up and all around.

# PART
# 4

The Hun hordes filled the scene as far as the eye could reach; however, there in that bend of the river, sunken rather deep between over-hanging bluffs, the eye could not reach very far. Emotion aboard the sailing-barge *Homoiousios* was in a state of flux. Augustus the Penurious, for example, even rose up a little ways off his bags of baggage and surveyed his captors with something like, first, surprise, and second, a rather cautious gratification. And in a moment, when one of the Huns rode, splashing, up to the side, his thin mouth open in a cruel and hungry leer, Augustus even rose to his full height as though the better to be seen. Then he gave a satisfied nod, and spoke.

"Hail," he said. "*Ave* Attila IV, Grand Hetman of the Hun Hordes, Scourge of God, King of Hun Horde Number Seventeen, and," and here he cleared his throat and gave a meaningful glance at the Hun on the horse, "and Ally of the Central Roman Empire. Hem."

The man so addressed seemed by no means totally pleased to have been identified so precisely. He rode even nearer, he squinted and scowled, then he spat.

"What?" he asked. "You Gustav Caesar Twenny-fi'?"

"Even so."

The Hun king plucked off his exceedingly greasy little fur bonnet and cast it into the water, and endeavored to direct his horse to trample on it. "Goddamn," he muttered. "Sunnamabitch Caesar, all-same ally. Rotten roundeyes fucken foreign-devil king. Oh,

sit. Horse-sit.'' Then he wheeled about to confront his
hordesmen, who had already begun to clamber up the
sides of the vessel, barking whinnying sounds in his
native tongue (if such it could be denominated; perhaps
palate or glottis would be better), breaking into the
common vernacular in another moment.

"No rob sip!" he yelled. "All-same ally sip. *Sit!*"

One of the hordesmen commencing to contend this
diplomatic decision, the King of Hun Horde Number
Seventeen at once whirled his flail and brought it down
with a *thunk* upon the man's skull. The man scowled
sullenly, slowly withdrew, ignoring the blood stream-
ing down onto his seamed face, whereon any number of
scars and scabs testified to past recalcitrancies. A mutter began among the horsemen, to whom the niceties of
the laws of nations perhaps meant less than to others.
Appledore at this point stepped forward, suddenly re-
assuming, for the first time since having left Sapodilla,
his role as *a capella* bard.

*I sing the curses of civilized men* [he sang] *Upon the
accursed Hordes of Huns, most Vile and most vicious
of vermin: Woe!*

The most vile and most vicious of vermin broke off
their muttering, and looked at the bard from their tiny
and blood-shot eyes, whilst small and appreciative
twitches began to play around the corners of their flat
mouths.

*Dreading to declare how they burned
The basilicas, I lift up my voice to
Mourn the moment they impaled priests
And benightedly buggered the bishops: Woe!*

The hordesmen simpered, looking around from under their scanty eyelashes. The dirty toes of Attila IV curled in his plaited-grass stirrups, and his lower lip thrust forward, he shuffled in his seat, and in general gave the impression that if he were on dry land he would have dug his toes into the ground in a pleasurable embarrassment at hearing himself praised.

> *Alas, how the inhuman Huns violated the*
> *Virgins, vigorously ignored their shrieks*
> *And crushed the craniums of the innocent*
> *Acolytes, like unto over-ripe apples: Woe!*

Attila IV giggled, broke out in a slight blush, and looked the rather helpless look of the innately modest man who is overcome at the mention of his own praises, and simply doesn't know which way to turn. Finally it was all too much for him, he broke forth into a delighted guffaw; then, summoning a stern gaze which tended to wobble a bit, he said, ''Enough, sing-song man. You sing plenty-good. Me gib you gift.'' He barked an order, and one of his men lifted himself slightly off what appeared to be a saddle done in red mauretanian leather, but which proved to be a steak of horse-meat, fibres well-tenderized beneath the Hun's half-breeched buttock; and handed it to Appledore. The best all-out *a capella* bard turned slightly green.

''I fear I have already breakfasted,'' he murmured, faintly. ''I shall save it for supper—if, even then, I can bring myself to part with such a token of the esteem of your Maleficent Majesty by eating it . . .''

The horsemen guffawed, and even His Maleficent Majesty smiled his amusement. ''You no likee,'' he said. ''Likee slabe food, bread and beef. Arright.'' At a gesture the horsemeat was removed from the bard's slack hands, and once again was transformed into a saddle. The horde-hetman's tiny red eyes moved to his fellow-monarch. "Caesar-king gib you six piecee gold instead," he said.

The caesar-king did indeed give Appledore six pieces of gold, but he moved as though he would have sooner parted with six fingers. At this Eugenius stepped forward and, raising high his hand, solemnly made the Sign of the Snake. The hordesmen reverently bowed their heads . . . briefly.

"What you want, Snake-sage?" asked their king.

"If the King would kindly have his men harness their horses to this vessel we may yet bring her off the sand-bank," the Eddessan suggested.

Attila IV, Grand Hetman of the Hun Hordes, Scourge of God, King of Hun Horde Number Seventeen, and Ally of the Central Roman Empire, scowled very suddenly, causing furrows to appear in the very narrow place between his scalp and his eyes. "What you think you hire teamsters, sunnamabitchgoddamn?" he enquired. "You makes insult? You never hear of Death of One Thousand Cuttees? By damn, maybe I makee spleen belonga you walkabout in fire too much!"

The Eddessan was very pale, but long years of facing menace at the hands of all sorts and qualities of men of all sorts of tribes and tongues had helped to harden him against present threat and danger. He said nothing, allowing the barbarian, not to say savage, monarch's own spleen to be vented as he might will. And, evidently there was much pent up in the Hun's organ. He began with the complaint that his reasonable and respectable offer of marriage to the sister-in-law's great-niece's cousin of some recently deceased caesar of the East had not even been received with the contumely and scorn which his own might and rank entitled him, but had been merely and unforgiveably ignored. He went on to complain that his share of the perpetual tribute which the Eparch of Pappadoupolis had promised his grandfather had been paid in unroasted pumpkin seeds instead of specie. He expressed his deep offense, not to say bitterness, that at his last attempt to enlist the Imperial support for which his status as an allied King entitled him in order to press his rightful claims to the kingship of Hun Horde Number Sixteen, the gatekeepers at Ravenna had suggested that he leave his name and return during the office hours for minor claimants. The list of grievances was long and complex, and ended with the grudging admission that of all the caesars with whom he had contact, only the one aboard, to wit Augustus XXV, had treated him with civility.

"And what he give me?" he demanded. "Parade! —You think I eat parade? You think I feed Hun Horde Sebenteem with Parade?"

The august caesar-in-exile (no one had thought it well to advise the Fourth Attila of Stingy Gus's recent change in status . . . or, at any rate, in residence) kept a diplomatic silence. Peregrine secretly sympathized with the bowlegged little king. Hun Horde Number Seventeen was probably not one of the larger Hun Hordes, indeed, by Peregrine's actual and silent count, it numbered a grand total of eleven men, two of whom were riding postern; plus three moldy-looking yourts now lumbering into view drawn by a scrawny ox a-piece. He was certain that something more than a parade must be needed to feed even such a small horde, and he rather marveled at King Attila's refusal, however reluctant, to allow any pillage of the vessel bearing someone whose technical status as ally had never resulted in anything more rewarding than a parade.

Still, Peregrine conceded, though Attila IV might

now be feeling only the non-nutritional value of a parade, it must be better than nothing, when you are a very small-gruel Hun king, at least to get every now and then a parade at no extra cost. It might be that something of this sort now entered the sorely-vexed mind of Attila, for he wound up his complaint by flinging at Eugenius the words, "You think you catchee great-grandchilds Attila the Great for pull your boat for penny-money?"

"Oh certainly not, Your Terrible Majesty," the Eddessan said, very promptly. "For I have just been obliged to declare a demurrage by virtue of our having been heavy-laden and grounded due to certain cargo, plus perils of other princes and potentates; and for the service I have been obliged to ask I would certainly not offend any of the great-grandchildren of Attila the Great by offering his men coppers for the assistance we need," and with that and ignoring the half-outraged, half-agonized looks of Stingy Gus, he kicked the nearest baggage-bag: and it clinked loudly.

With little more delay the hordesmen pressed not only their horses but their three boney oxen into the task of dislodging the *Homoiousios* from the sandbar—in fact, they even bent their own wiry bodies into the task, accompanied by a cheerful, wailing chant which—so their king informed the foreigners—commemorated the burning of a basilica in South Burgundy with the entire congregation still inside: and whenever they showed signs of languishing, Eugenius would give the moneybags another kick, Augustus the Penurious would wince, and Hun Horde Number Seventeen would throw itself and its beasts with renewed zeal into the task at hand.

At length the barge floated freely once more, its captain collected his demurrages and his penalties, the

Horde was paid its honorarium, and almost everybody was and looked very pleased.

"Attila keepee word," said Attila. "Attila no lootee, no killee, no rapee, all-same everysing sip-sape."

At mention of the last horror from which the Hun King had abstained, Sister Pulchrituda started, and seemed to emerge from a revery. "Far be it from *me,*" she now said, coming forward, "to stand between the terrible Huns and their customary customs."

Matron Eudoxia made a grab for her, but even before she caught her, the King of the Huns had made his final judgement. "You too skinny," he said. But some thought had evidently entered his mind, sparked, perhaps, by Pulchrituda's words, and perhaps partly by Eudoxia's gesture. Her it was whom he addressed next.

"Hey! Fat Roman Mamma!" he said. "You likee eat Hun food?"

Eudoxia heaved a huge sigh, and gave Peregrine a sidelong glance. "Oh, the tribulations which a Christian must expect to endure in this vale of tears!" she observed. And, in an undertone, "It would be a sheer shame to allow all of that good gold to remain in the hands of the unregenerate. —Girls!" she said, crisply, pushing her hair-do into place, "—Company!"

\*   \*   \*   \*

There was no wind, and, for the moment at least, no one seemed to feel the need of one. The barge floated slowly down the river. Hun Horde Number Seventeen—or part of it, anyway—ambling in the shallows and keeping up with her. The yourts lurched behind, and from them came an occasional whoop, hoot, or yell intended to be blood-curdling; also, now and then, a rather ladylike scream, and sometimes even a giggle.

Eugenius was keeping his eyes, and perhaps, by his silence, his mind, strictly on the work of navigation. Appledore had broached a keg of soused beef and was restoring his energies, depleted as they had been by his unwonted exertions as *a capella* bard. Stingy Gus, long deep in thought, now beckoned to Peregrine, who, nothing loath, approached the ex-ruler of Nimrunna.

"Young man," said the latter, "you seem to be the most sensible person aboard this floating circus, except of course for myself. I have observed you engaged in the productive task of sharpening your sword, for example. Also, I recollect with respect how you declined to accept for your Imperial scrip the price which the Bursary in its official capacity was obliged to offer. A fool and his money are soon parted, as I believe Homer remarks somewhere, or is it the Proverbs of King Solomon? No matter; and I am no fool, Nor, I believe, are you."

Peregrine received these comments in a respectful silence, but said nothing, believing them in any event to be prolegomenal in nature. A short space of time proved him right in this respect. For a moment he and the other observed some water-fowl take wing abaft their seats, trailing their feet in the water a good ways before leaving it entirely. Then the older man lifted his gaze from the birds' wake and continued.

"I found Nimrunna a mere non-place," he said, "and in a short while I had made it a hive of industry and commerce worthy of being the seat of a Caesar. Perhaps I was too severe. It may be so. I ought to have allowed more for the flighty side of man's nature. After all, man liveth not by bread and brothels alone. So be it. I am not too old to learn. I was intended by Providence to be a Caesar, and a Caesar I shall be; if not in

Nimrunna, then elsewhere. I have the capacity, and equally to the point, I have—despite the extortions of that snake-snuggling woolmonger—I have the funds. But I have not the folly to think I can begin anew if I begin alone.

"How would you like," he asked abruptly, "to be the General of my Armies?"

Peregrine blinked. "Of your *what?*"

"Come, don't play the fool. 'Of my Armies,' is what I said. True, I haven't a single foot-slogger right now, let alone a single cohort. But what of that? Neither did I have when I first started out. Anyone who can pay soldiers' wages can find soldiers to follow him. Well. Enough time-wasting. Do you think you'd like that?"

Peregrine said, "I think that I might like it very much indeed. Of course," he said, more slowly, "that might depend on what terms . . ."

"Five bezants a year, and all found," said Augustus, promptly.

The putative General of the Armies wiggled a finger in an ear and examined it. "Must clean them better," he commented. "Thought you said 'five.' Amusing isn't it? When of course what you said was 'five hundred' . . . wasn't it?"

The jaw of Augustus sank till Peregrine would have thought it could sink no lower, yet it sank still lower; and as it sank, so did his eyebrows raise. "Before whom do you think you stand?" he asked, wonderingly. "Before the very Emperor Himself, by whose hands and mint the very bezants themselves are coined?"

Peregrine looked at him coolly. "I might be standing," he said, slowly and thoughtfully, "before the future very Emperor Himself, by whose hands and mint the very bezants themselves are coined."

The jaw of Augustus slowly raised, slowly met its

upper, and slowly they clamped together, tightly, tightly, and ever more tightly; as though he were pressing out bezants in a die between his teeth; his eyes became narrower and narrower until they were two slits. He surveyed the young man before him in a silence which was not broken for some still moments.

"Young man," he then said, "You have youth, audacity, cunning, courage, and a total absence of scruples. *I like your spirit*. Five hundred bezants a year, then."

"And all found," Peregrine added, promptly.

But he had perhaps gone too far. "With Caesar, one does not quibble over cheese and shoe-laces," said Caesar, loftily. And rose, and drew his cloak around him. "Bring up the ship's chart," he directed. "And let us consider the lay of the land."

*    *    *    *

Peregrine had gone ashore to attend to a private need which could be more privately attended to than aboard, and was walking lazily after the sailing-barge as it floated downstream with its sail limp, when he heard a hiss. He jumped without thinking, then carefully scanned the ground, but no serpent did he see. The hiss came again, and this time he identified its source as a thicket nearby, and he was eyeing the brush with a mixture of suspicion and annoyance, when its branches were slightly parted and a face peered out at him. It was Claud.

"Pssst! In here," he said, and thrust out a hand of which one finger wiggled back towards him. Peregrine shrugged, and, the bush being parted more lightly, made his way into it.

"So you escaped, too," said Claud.

Peregrine stared at him a moment, then burst out into

laughter. Claud, not sharing in his merriment, asked what was the joke. It took some moments of explanation, and Claud did not seem as gratified as one might perhaps think he should have been to hear that his friends had escaped torture and massacre. Peregrine, though vaguely aware of his companion's nonpresence recently, had in truth quite forgotten its cause; though he did not think it judicious to mention that.

"Well," said Claud, thinking things over. "Well," he said again, "I'm glad that everything's all right. Philoxena and I were sure worried." Philoxena gave Peregrine a glance, and tossed a mischievous lock of hair over her shoulder. If she had indeed been worrying, no traces of it now showed. She looked, in fact, very content.

"Seems like you've been more or less having a kind of picnic on the palace lawn," said Claud, slightly resentfully. "I hope there were enough hard-boiled eggs."

Peregrine thought it time to divert this trend of thought. "How would you like a position on the staff of a very highly-placed military officer?" he asked.

"A very highly-placed *what?*"

"You may address me henceforth," Peregrine said, carelessly, "as General Peregrine. *Strategos*, to be formal, oh, but let's not be formal. In fact, unless we are actually in uniform, skip the title altogether."

"What in the hell are you talking about?" It was explained to him. He scowled, tousled his hair, looked at his friend with a suspicious look, then said, "Well, if you say so."

"I do say so."

"I suppose he's got the money, all right."

"He certainly does have the money all right."

Claud shrugged his acceptance of the situation, began to rise, then settled down again, and again he scowled. It was going to be rather embarrassing, he explained, to return to the ship just then. "Under the circumstances," he said. And he looked rather sheepish. Philoxena looked anything but sheepish.

"Why must we go back?" she asked. "I not wanting to go back. Hun men smelling too badly." The implication struck Claud very forcefully, and he, with a renewed scowl, put his arm around her, and she snuggled contentedly under it.

"Oh, I don't want you to go back just now," said Peregrine. "In fact your being as you are can work out very well, I think. Just kind of keep the boat in sight, keeping out of sight yourselves, though. You're going to be my Chief of Scouts, at least for the time being." He opened his pouch. "Here is Caesar's bread and salt," he said, breaking off and dipping and handing over. "Do you accept?"

"I accept."

"Well, what I want you to do is to keep your eyes and your ears open. And each morning and each evening, when the sun is about so high, or so low, I'll contrive to meet you. You can just hiss again, like before—"

Claud was already well into the mood. "Yes, that was very good, the way I hissed," he said, complacently. "Got your attention right away, didn't it. —Go ahead, go ahead," he said, hastily. "I'm listening . . . very carefully."

"And report to me of your movements and of your observations. Of men and beasts and birds, of walls and gates, of lands and waters, of all things which occur in the daytime and of all things which pass in the night. —Here's your first pay, and here's your first advance on expenses; don't be too ostentatious in the way you spend any of it, and be careful of how you draw attention to yourself."

Deeply impressed, Claud said, "Yes, General— I mean, Perry. And, uh, what else?"

Peregrine considered a moment, but could think of nothing else. "That will be all for now," he said, somewhat grandly. Philoxena gave him a grateful glance. It may have been that she, for one, had thought of something else.

The boat had floated some ways downstream, and Peregrine had to run to catch up with it.

Appledore greeted him. "Stretching your legs, eh? I don't blame you. Mine, however, have had all the stretching they need during our recent journeyings on foot, and I'm glad to let them contract. —Say, the next real city ahead should be Chinigirium, if I'm not mistaken. It used to be on a west branch of the river, but that one dried up; fortunately the east branch flowed right past the other end of town so they just had to build new docks."

"Is that so?" said Peregrine, lazily, who had seen the chart.

"Yes, it is. And what's more to the point, an old and very dear schoolmate of mine is there, or used to be: the philosopher Volumnius. You wouldn't have guessed it, though, at one time, that he would ever get to be a philosopher!"

"Is that so?"

"Yes, it is. In fact, in those days we used to call him the Dumb Ass of Parnassus! Ha ha ha! What do you think of that for a nickname?"

He paused, and Peregrine, who had not been closely attending, but, observing the expectant pause and politely desiring to return an answer, hazarded, "The Child of Abraxas . . ."

"Ha ha, not quite. Volumnius came of middle-class parents in the provincial city of N. Funny name for a city, isn't it?"

Instead of attempting an answer, and the question in fact, hardly seeming to need any, Peregrine spoke on something which he had just been reminded of. "Say, Appledore, *about* the child of Abraxas, and that spell by which you re-created him?" "What about it my boy?" "Well, it just occurred to me that I once saw a gemstone ring which my old uncle Bumbulac used to have, and there was an Abraxas on it: *You* called him in your spell, 'Ass-headed Abraxas,' right? —but on this ring I saw once he had a cock's head."

Appledore politely raised his brows, arose and gave his limbs a comfortable if limited stretch. "Did you, my boy? Did it? Did he? Well . . . The spell *worked*, didn't it? So I must have gotten *some*thing right?"

Thin cool shafts of sunlight were passing through the trees along the riverbanks when Eugenius decided to tie up for the night. A similar thought occurred to the Hun Hordes, or, at any rate, to Hun Horde Number Seventeen, for the yourts came to a slow and lurching stop in the flats not far from the boat. Peregrine ambled over, passing Matron Eudoxia and ladies, who murmured something to him about Christian resignation, vales of tears, missionary efforts among the heathen, future purchases of holy oil for holy lamps; and would perhaps have murmured more to him about something else, save for a slight twinge which caught her when she half-turned; so that what she actually said was, "Christos Chrestos, I'm sore. I don't believe them goddam Huns sweep the gravel out of those lop-sided bee-hives from one year's end to another! Furthermore, I'm hungry, and I don't mean for any more chop horsey, either, I want some Christian vittles such as bread and beef. Well . . . see you later, then, prettyboy . . ."

The lady-Huns who were preparing the campfires (although what they might cook thereon, Peregrine could not imagine) ignored him as he came up. Attila

IV gestured towards a horsehide rug near his own, and Peregrine sat, crossing his legs as the other was doing—a gesture which did not escape his host. "Hoy," he said. "You sittee on ground all-same Hun sittee, not like Christian."

"Well, I'll tell you a secret, King. I'm not really a Christian."

The Hun digested his slowly. Then he slowly nodded. "Secret, yes. Me no tellee. But no tell white man, you! Hammer big sharp stick up—"

"I know, I know. Boy, do I know!"

His host sighed deeply. "Sunamabitch big goddamn day. Me all tire out. You know gamboo-game, play with knuckoo-bone? Yes? Fat white mamma lady show how, catchee allee money from ship captain gib us. Now me number one poor boy again. Me! Attila Four, Grand Hetman Hun Hordes, Scourgee God, King Hun Horde Number Sebemteem . . ." He passed into a moody silence, then, the traditional hospitality of the nomad (ha!) breaking even into his moodiness, he ran his hand through an open sackful of something which Peregrine could not at once identify: "Likee pumpkin seed?" the Scourge of God inquired, listlessly. "Raw . . . Good for keepee peepee up," he added, with a graphic gesture. He heaved a huge sigh, which, as it progressed, contained notes which were on the whole not entirely without contentment.

"Listen, King," Peregrine said, leaning forward, Attila at once stifled his yawn, leaned towards his guest. "Do any of the peoples down the river know that you and your people are here?"

Attila thought about this, his hairline almost meeting his eyebrows as he concentrated. Then he drew something which might, with both generosity and imagination, be called a map, in the sand with an exceedingly grubby great-toe. "Lessee . . . Horde come from *here*

. . . Ribber runnee ober *here* . . . *Down* ribber down *dere* . . .'' He withdrew a bit and examined his carto- graphical exercise with a measure of fondness. Rapidly he cast up the whole thing in his mind, discerned an answer.

''Nope. No-boddee know. Wha'-fo you ask?''

Peregrine brought his hand fairly close to the other's tiny rufous eyes, and showed him the band of a thin and flat and rather worn ring. Then he revolved it. On the bezel, no longer concealed, was the stag's-head symbol of Sapodilla. And over it was a crown. Attila scowled, considering. A stag's head by the bezel's brim, a sim- ple stag's head was to him; but a crown was, after all, a crown.

''Hey,'' he commented. ''What? You King? Lillee boy like you, king?''

Peregrine said, quite truthfully, ''No. My father is a king.''

There may have been times when Attila's mind moved slowly, but these times were not every time. ''Then what you do here?'' he asked. And at once answered his own question. ''Ho. You get chase out. You bahrstar, huh?'' Peregrine nodded. The savage little chieftain clapped him on the back. ''Nevva mine,'' he said. ''You no Christian, me no Christian, we no givee fuck.'' He lifted his head, and uttered some sounds which were half-whinnies and half-clicks. One of the lady-Huns rose and removed from the fire some- thing which sizzled and dripped. Something shifted uneasily in Peregrine's innards. Was this, he won- dered, the same saddle of horsemeat which had twice changed hands, so to speak, earlier that day? He had an unwholesome vision of it, progressing halfway across lower central Europe at a slow trot, getting softer and softer.

''You no mine eatee woman food,'' said King Attila

indulgently. It was almost certainly horse, for surely that rib had never formed part of ox or cow; it was, however, quiet definitely a rib, and he could hardly imagine the most case-hardened Hun riding very far on top of it. And also, remembering the bawdy tale of the young first Caesar and the King of Pontus, he was thankful that no grosser (or more limber) item of anatomy was now being thrust at him. He thanked his host, took it by the stick which impaled it, and began to nibble.

It was of course tough and it lacked the smoothness of mutton, veal, or beef; it was slightly sweetish. But he was young and he was hungry and he was diplomatic; and it was not bad. After several minutes of champing, he propped the bit up where the fire would finish cooking the inside portion of it. "Listen, King," he said, again, "how would you like to collect some tribute?"

The red little eyes gleamed in the red firelight.

"Listen, King-son," he countered, "wouldee bear sit in the woods?"

"Well . . ."

"Who you want kill?"

"Well . . ."

"Where he live?"

The other members of Hun Horde Number Seventeen may not have known even much dog-Latin, but their leader's only semi-suppressed enthusiasm communicated its own message. They came slinking and gathering round about like wolves. Their tongues almost overlapped their lips. Likewise their eyes gleamed. And, remembering a lair he had briefly entered one winter hunt with his brother Austin, Peregrine decided that they even smelled like wolves.

"I want you to fall behind the boat," he said. "I want you, though, to have out at least one scout who will always keep the boat in sight. I would like your main horde to keep out of sight as much as possible. Right now we are still in hilly country, woods—but very soon the tilled places will start. I wish that you, King, will see to it that no raiding at all is done . . . not so much as a pigeon from a cote . . . don't even burn a hay-stack. Will it be so?''

Some dog-Latin some of the hordesmen certainly knew, for these harsh conditions produced a certain amount of restlessness in their ranks. But, their chief glancing up then and the fire glinting upon his cheeks where once long ago a red-hot iron had seared the flesh to kill the hair, the mere look itself was like a red-hot iron: and at that moment he was very King and Scourge indeed; and Peregrine thought that he looked, not like a wolf— Like a tiger.

"So," said Peregrine.

"*Very* so," said Attila the King.

His new-made ally knew just where his thoughts were. "You meetee me. I meetee you. We make talkee-talkee. Not so?''

"Even so.''

"*Very* so," said Attila the King. "Sunumabitch, *yes*.''

\*    \*    \*    \*

Augustus said, "I confess that the presence of the Huns makes me somewhat unhappy. They are a singularly non-productive people. I thought it wisest, back in Nimrunna, to conciliate them with pomps and ceremonies. But it is difficult to do that without a city at one's immediate disposal. I suppose they did come in somewhat handy today, floating this wretched tub off, ungodly costly though it was. However, I should like to be able to hope not to see them tomorrow.''

Peregrine said, "I can guarantee that we won't."

"You *can?* Good! How do you know? Oh. Oh *ho*.
You arranged that, did you? Very good. How did
you— Well, I shan't ask that. Sent them back to raid
and pillage Nimrunna, I suppose. What I was thinking
of, myself." He gave a thin, wheezing chuckle. "Well
done. *Very* well done, in fact, General."

"Thank you, Sire," said Peregrine.

*   *   *   *

Day after day the vessel ambled down the river,
seeing no other. Now and then, slowly increasing in
number, they saw the smoke of hearth-fires: but always
afar off, as, where there were not hills by the bankside
there were often bogs and swamps. And once, Matron
Eudoxia, rousing herself from the comfortable doze
which was her usual condition, flowed to the side and
said that if she didn't swear to Holy Wisdom, but if that
there to the left didn't look like a *sudd!* —and this, she
explained, was a sort of conglomerate of land and water
and vegetation to which the waterways of Nubia were
inclined to be sogged and sometimes clogged and
swamped with. But what with the warmth and stillness,
no one was inclined to pursue the matter.

Eugenius was all intent on piloting his ship through
the mazy channels. Augustus sat upon his bags of
bezants as though on a throne, dreaming dreams of
glory and productive industry. Appledore had redis-
covered the tattered pages first found in the junkyard of
Ulrich the ironmonger, and alternatively frowned and
mumbled as he slowly scanned them. Sister Pulchrituda, doubtless out of long, long habit, tended to
the fire.

No one was moved to question Peregrine's habit of
leaving the boat for varying periods of time. Morning

and evening, he met with Claud (and sometimes Philozena) on the left bank; always, at noontime, he met with King Attila on the right. Claud had ceased to make any complaints about the heaviness of prongs, or, for that matter, about anything else. Attila, however—whose command of the common tongue was improving with use—had many complaints . . . or, rather, one complaint, on which he rang changes.

''Bread and beef, bread and beef, and beef and bread: food for slabes eatee, for slabes, Boy, food. Givee man fine fillet ten-year-old stallion, with paprika sprinkle and rubbee garlic, puttee between horses and Hun and makee tender by ten-twennee mile gallop, ahah and ahah and yoy, Boy! Food fittee for eat! Fittee for eat, food!'' And he smacked his cracked and chapped lips and licked the dust off them with a coated and gummy tongue. Howsomever, ''All-same quiet,'' he reported on the right bank. Curiously enough, on the left, Claude also mentioned that useful beast, the horse.

''That's why I got the new clothes,'' he explained, somewhat defensively. ''The ones I had were only good enough for a thrall,'' he said, ''but when I explained to the farmer that my horse had been stolen with the real good ones in the saddle bags, he swallowed it—sold me these extra Sunday-go-to-market duds he had. So it occurred to me, 'This is it!' ''

''This is *what?*'' Peregrine queried.

''My *cover*, see? I'm a farmer from out of the district trying to locate my strayed or stolen horse. Couldn't go around looking like it was *me* that'd run away, could I? I might be seized for a reward—''

Peregrine felt twinges of guilt. He had never given a thought as to how Claud was dressed, or how he might feel about how he was dressed, or of anything of his thoughts or feelings. ''Listen, Chief of Scouts,'' he said, "as long as you stop short of purple, nobody on the staff cares how well you dress."

"And furthermore, it's an ideal was to get conversation started. You describe the animal, see—'He's a roan with a white stocking,' as it might be. No, says Agricolus, he hasn't seen any horse like *that*, but he tells you about some roans he *has* seen, then he mentions other horses with white stockings he's seen. Next thing you know he starts talking about any suspicious-looking strangers he's seen . . . . Before you know it, you got a pretty good idea of all the movements going on in the district."

Peregrine nodded. "That sounds like a sound way of going about it. Well. And what movements have been going on in the district, then?"

Claud, who had brightened, un-brightened. He looked away and kicked pebbles. "Well, as a matter of fact, *no* movements have been going on in the district," he admitted. "But if there ever *are*, I bet you I get to hear about them!"

The General Staff was feeling slightly stale about events in general when he clambered aboard the *Homoiousios* once more. "Anything of interest in your old papyruses, Doctor Appledore?" he asked without much expectations.

"Oh, it's all interesting, my boy, but on the whole it's all inconclusive, too. The pages appear to have formed part of a sort of commonplace book, or codex of random notes, as kept by someone called either Epiglottis of Epizoötic, or Epizoötic of Epiglottis— interpreted *one* way. Interpreted *another* way, both words could form part of a treatise on veterinary medicine. And then there's *this* phrase, which puzzled me for two whole days, *Hunc nunc tibi bibi bubu pupu pipi tipi*—but then I figured out that he was just testing his pen. And then, for example, there's this. *Tiberius expelled them from Rome because Chrestus was always inciting them to violence*. And—''

Languidly interested, Peregrine said, "A mistake, clearly for Christus, I would suppose."

Appledore gave the delighted snort of a pedant who has caught someone in error. "You would, would you? Then you'd be wrong. Chrestus is a Latin form of the Greek for *righteous*, and the phrase, I clearly remember, is from Tacitus. Refers, supposedly, to the Jews; probably intended to refer to the early Christians. And then we have this: *Say that it is blasphemous to talk of separating the sheep from the goats, for the sheep and the goat are one*. Should have read Aristotle on the Categories. And, oh, just picking at random, a question as to, was the *morbus divus* the same as the *morbus demoniacus* and if so, was it from God or from the Devil, which? That is, the dreaded falling sickness, as the folk call it . . . shriek, convulsion, unconsciousness . . . in a word, epilepsy. Also—it notes—called *morbus comitialis*, because if anyone was seized during any public or official gathering, said convocation automatically dissolved. Then comes a receipt for how to mummify cats, in your basement—very useful, I'm sure, if you ever have a cat you want mummified cheap. And just all sorts of goodies like that . . ."

He looked at his former pupil with tired, kindly eyes. "But why should you be interested in such a budget of dead-men's bones, my boy? Perk up, this voyage will soon come to an end, or, at least, this leg of it. Big port ahead; singing and dancing, and something better to eat and drink than ship's stores pickled in sheep-stink. And if things prove peaceful and remain so, perhaps we'll get our land legs back again."

Peregrine grunted, mumbled that perhaps he'd even,

somehow, be able to send a letter back to his dadda.

Appledore snapped his fingers, slapped his brow, and got up, rather hastily. "I clean forgot! And not only that—I clean forgot to tell you—strictest confidence, of course—I've been engaged as Augur, part-time and *pro tem*, by—but I don't know that I can disclose that just yet. Excuse me. Be back in a jiffy." He scuttled off, muttering as he went. "Favorable auspices from north-north-west, with aspects similar for tomorrow. Favorable—"

Peregrine stretched out, then rolled over, with his head cradled in his arms, and (slowly, slowly) relaxed.

*What think you, Brother?*

*It may be so. The day is not yet done, nor the shadows fled away.*

*After the shadows flee away, comes the greater shadow which is Night.*

*This tablet is as yet clean—think you not?*

*It is cleaner than most—no more.*

*What see you there, then?*

*I see hunger and thirst and venery.*

*He is a man, Brother.*

*As he is now, so once were we.*

*What think you, Brother?*

*I would wait, Brother, I would yet wait . . .*

Peregrine stirred, muttered, then once more fell silent.

He was awakened by the blaze of noon, slipped into the water full-clothed and refreshed himself, then walked along the shore and let the clothes dry on him. Presently he heard the nicker of the signal of the Huns, and he turned aside in its direction. There was Attila, and there were two of his men and someone between them, half on the ground and still struggling.

The Allied King said, succinctly, "Catchee spy."

"I deny it!" a somewhat muffled voice declared. "I deny the allegation, and I defy the allegator. Unhand me, heathen hound!"

"Let's see him," Peregrine said.

"Him" proved to be a portly, bearded man somewhat dustier for his encounter with the Hordesmen. "Let's hear some I.D., please," said the Chief of Staff.

"Would you prefer it in iambic pentameter, or in Corinthian?" queried the captive. Peregrine to this making no answer, the man went on to say that he was P. Cato Decimus Brutus Darlangius Philipus G., "And a member of the Imperial Senate, so have a care, sir. You will have a care, won't you?" He patted his pouch, shrugged. "Pardon. I would gladly have offered you one, but I seem to have left them all behind. Ah, well." He scanned the younger man, not seeming much incommoded by the circumstances of the meeting. "Ah, yes, the face is familiar; however, last year's model was taller, broader, and blonder . . . and you should have seen some of the broads, too." Senator P. C.D.B. Darlangius P.G. smacked his lips and winked. "Let me see," he continued. "Your name was certainly mentioned over more than one flagon of falernian. Haggard? Tiercel? Gyrfalcon? No, no, none of those. Shall we try for the sixty-four sesterces? *Peregrine?*"

"What—? Who—? How—?"

The senator smiled at the effect he had produced, an indication of assurance which did not please the little king, who growled, "Talkee-talkee all-same too muchee. We makee sharp stick, hammer up—" The senator's face showed an alarm which he perhaps did not entirely feel; nevertheless, he placed his hands against his well-rounded posterior.

"Little Brother," he said, "you have impetuous pals."

At which Peregrine's face lit up, and all—or at least some—became clear. "Austin! You know my brother Austin!"

"I do indeed know your brother Austin. We spent some very pleasant times together a while back. Indeed, I offered to use my best efforts to have him placed as Senator for the First Ward, West, in Chiringirium. But some absurd religious compunctions restrained him . . . . My dear boy, I am really very pleased to meet you. Er," he circled around so that his back was no longer to the Huns, and said, "won't you please assure your right honorable and gallant friends that—"

Peregrine gestured. "Yes, that's all right," he said, rather to the disappointment of his right honorable and gallant friends; "he really is a friend of my brother's." The Huns grumbled, but cantered off. Peregrine observed that one of them was tenderizing another steak . . . or perhaps it was still the same one. "But before we go into that," said Peregrine, "would you mind telling me what you were doing when they found you? It is still rather far from your city."

The full and full-bearded face of Senator Darlangius Philipus went suavely blank. He waved his hand. "My vast estates lie over there. That is to say, they used to. That is to say, the estates are still there where they always were, though now forming the property of a tax-farmer named Macromius, with whose wife—a lady of impeccable piety—I was discussing some alternative readings in various verses of the longer Psalms, when her husband unexpectedly arrived. The citizen Macromius is, shall we say, a man not over-friendly to book-learning—book-*keep*ing, yes. —You understand, my boy. On receiving news of his close arrival, I felt my presence to be superfluous. And, as I had been conveyed thither in the litter of the Lady Macromius

. . .'' He waved his hand. Further explanation, the gesture implied, would be tedious . . . and, between men of the world, unnecessary.

He placed his hand on the younger man's shoulder as they walked along, and he talked of Austin, who (Peregrine was disappointed, but not surprised to hear) had moved on, almost a year ago. Peregrine gathered that the decline in the Senator's personal fortunes, occasioned by such factors as bad crops, the competition of foreign grain, high taxes, malevolence in high places, jealousy in low, over-confidence and excessive generosity; the Senator bore with a truly Christian resignation. ''Of my wounds suffered in my country's wars, my descent from Patricius Platus who slew the outlaw Guillermus Haedus, I say nothing. *Sic friatur crustulum*, as Ovid puts it; 'Thus,' or, 'In that matter, does the cookie crumble.' I have, after all, my collection of first editions of the Patristic Fathers; I have a certain amusing skill in games, an ear for good poetry, an eye for good women—'Good,' a purely subjective term, anyway, as Aristotle would be the first to concede, delicious pilaffs he used to make, but his baklava was a bit too sticky—if there is any thing I abhore more than another it is having to pause in the middle of a philosophical discussion to lick honey off my fingers . . . Where was I? Ah yes. Licking honey. Just so. Yes, your big brother and I had a very pleasant time together, but he felt he had to move on. There was a certain man in high office—Observe that I do not, I repeat, *not*, denominate our noble Caesar, C. Petronius Niger, sometimes called Black Pete—who has a tendency to glance askance at men of verve and capacity, unless they have the good sense to play themselves down; and Austin wouldn't, you know, he just *wouldn't*. So he left. Smart boy. You look very much like him.''

He took another and a closer look at Peregrine, and something seemed genuinely to trouble him. "In fact," he said, "to someone who hadn't observed Austin closely, and day after day, as I did, someone of a narrow and shallow and suspicious mind . . . the idea might occur that *you* are Austin . . . with your hair dyed, say . . . in hopes of avoiding the sentence of outlawry which," he sighed, "I very much regret to say was pronounced against him shortly after his absence was discovered when the soldiers called at the house of a lady of high birth to whom a certain person in high office is known also to favor. —He got away safe, in other words."

The senator went on to say, in more words, that just such a narrow, shallow, and suspicious mind was possessed by the Prefect of the Port, one Bruton, "Who used to be the Public Torturer, till he gave the profession a bad name: and now patrols the port with a sharp eye and a hungry look. Me, he ignores. Who, after all, would proclaim in the Senate the virtues of National Wet Dream Week, or whatever babblement it may be, if not for me? But *you*, my boy . . ." He shook his head. "You must skip the town altogether. Skulk through the old river bed and meet your friends' vessel, that you mention, below the City.

"But, I beg of you, don't hazard the docks."

Peregrine nodded thoughtfully.

"That's what I'll have to do, then, I guess. And . . . well . . . since it seems as if I may well have to miss this city, where my brother passed so much time, so much of it pleasantly, won't you at least tell me all about it? We can discuss it over lunch. It's only ships' stores, you know, beef and bread and wine and all from the barrels; and I marked the place where I'd put it with a strip of cloth—there it is!"

Senator P. Cato Decimus Brutus Darlangius Philipus

G. sank onto a hummock in the shade of a drupe tree with a small sound to which the word "grunt" could not be applied, unless, of course, with great measure of terminological exactitude. "No apologies for simple sailor fare is needed," he said. "*Et ego in Arcadia*, and so on. A corned beef sandwich! And is that celery tonic? No, it is wine. Ah well, mustn't grumble, Pour it carefully, my boy." He sipped, softly smacked his lips. Then he smiled.

"It's only a small domestic falernia," he said. "But I think we'll be amused at its naive presumption."

And, after another moment, "Tell you all about the City, eh? *Very* well."

An hour passed pleasantly, with Senator Darlangius Philipus discoursing on the City, and now and then illustrating a point with a quickly sketched diagram, and Peregrine, chin propped on fists, watching and listening. "Pity you hadn't brought along more of this good, small wine," said the senator. "However, we must husband our resources, and then, you say, there is more aboard. The Pus and Thistle, I mean the Thrush and Whistle, has a wine not unlike this one—a little wine-shop right behind the Church of Saint Stephanos, commonly called Smokey Steve's; whether the arch-priest has something to hide, or whether he's merely a latent pyromaniac, compensating, I don't know, but he certainly shovels on the incense, great billowing clouds of it at every mass, from nave to narthex.

"After the Senate closes for the day—and one of the very few compensations of being its president, as I happen to be this term, is that if a session shows signs of being unduly prolonged, I can close it with a rap of my ivory gavel—say, if I have an appointment to discuss ecclesiastical architecture with a pious matron, with emphasis on the Perpendicular Style, of course—and if not, because my throat sometimes grows quite dry from eloquence, I drop by Smokey Steve's to catch the late morning mass, where, of course, the incense only makes it *dry*er, and the arch-priest snatches the chalice away as though wine were going out of style; fortunately, as I have just explained, the Thrush and Whistle is right nearby. And so one can take a little wine for one's stomach sake, and for one's often infirmities: and to pick up the latest rumor going around—''

He rolled a mouthful of the domestic Dalmatia from tongue to palate, and gave a faint and grateful sigh.

''And speaking of rumor,'' he said, ''you've probably heard something as you've come down stream, of this great rebel fleet upstream?''

Peregrine lifted his chin. ''*What* great rebel fleet upstream?''

Senator D. allowed a gentle eructation to pass his lips with only the faintest expression of surprise; when it was followed by another, he at once converted it into a benediction, ''*Cum* spiritus tuum,'' he murmured. ''There. I might have known it was all nothing but scuttlebutt. Well, according to the stories, there have been all kinds of unrest in the Up Country. Heresy riots in one place, galleys sunk in another, a caesar overturned in a third. *You* know the sort of thing. Accompanied by talk of omens. Three-headed poontangs born in one place, strange lights seen in another, mummified martyrs move their heads and groan. I take it all with many a grain of salt. Heard it all before, *ov*er and over. But it tends to make Black Pete nervous, you know. And when Caesar says it's hot, the Senate sweats.''

He turned the wine-jar over and caught the sole remaining drop on the tip of a finger, and tasted it. Then he slowly and with grave dignity rose to his feet in stages. ''I fear that your friends must by this time be feeling concerned about you,'' he said. ''It would be the grossest selfishness on my part to oblige you to

return unescorted through strange terrain and coun-
tryside.''

And, Peregrine, after checking the sun, suggesting
that some fast walking might be in order, in order to
catch up with the vessel, Senator P. Cato Decimus
Darlangius Philipus G. expressed a pious hope that he
might be mistaken.

And he was.

\*     \*     \*     \*

Philoxena was aboard and hysterical, and continu-
ously attempted to pull handfuls of her hair out by the
roots, or to leap over the side of the boat, or to beat her
head against the deck; and she had already torn bloody
marks upon the sides of her face with her fingernails.
Her body, however, bore other brutal marks and
wounds whose position was such that they could not
have been self-inflicted. The other women, loudly
wailing, now hovered over her tenderly, and now
seized and restrained her when the wildness of her grief
grew fiercer.

"What's happened?" cried Peregrine. And immediately asked a second question, knowing that one
answer had to do for both. "Where is Claud?"

Philoxena at once ceased her attempts to inflict more
damage upon herself, looked up at him, and burst out
weeping.

"Give the poor girl a cup of wine," suggested
Senator Darlangius. "In fact, give her two." And
emphasized the exceedingly warm-hearted nature of
his suggestion by resting one hand on the posterior of
the Matron Eudoxia, and the other in her bosom: then
withdrew them, so as not to impede her carrying out his

recommendation. Wine was brought—two cups of it—and Philoxena was induced to accept one of them. She sipped, sobbed, hiccoughed, and finally, setting down her cup, began to tell her story.

Claud had been captured.

"By the Huns?" exclaimed Peregrine, about to curse the excessive zeal which had brought about two useless captures in one short space of time. But it was not so, for Claud had been captured by soldiers, while he and Philoxena had been amiably talking about horses to a small farmer in the hills above the river. He was a stranger, he had no papers; obviously he was a spy the soldiers said—probably a spy for the rebel forces which had already executed so much dramatic action along the upper river. There was a movement to execute then and there the sentence of death which hangs automatically over all spies, but the sergeant in charge was insistent: Claud had, in effect, spied on Caesar, therefore unto Caesar he would go. And they had bound his arms and dragged him away.

Philoxena was under no illusions that, once he was within the city walls, there would be any talk of regrettable errors, followed by immediate release. And, as she had nothing else to offer in order to prevent his being taken within those city walls, she had offered herself. The soldiers had taken her, true—and roughly—but then they started off once more, Claud still captive. Here was where Philoxena must have first become hysterical, and that was when she must have incurred the greater part of her wounds. At last, either from a blow severe enough to bring her to her senses, or from a latent realization that she herself could accomplish nothing, she lay where she had been flung. And, the soldiers being gone, had made her way to the riverside, half-staggering and half-crawling—had seen

the small barge—and, by ripping off what was left of
her dress, and waving it, had attracted the attention of
those aboard.

"Senator, can you do anything about this?" asked
Peregrine. "You know the Caesar—"

Darlangius shook his head. "I *do* know the Caesar. I
do indeed. I know him far too well to think that any
intercession of mine could effect the release of anyone
charged with peddling pistachios without a license—let
alone someone suspected of a major threat to the
Caesar's throne. I am sorry. I am very sorry. You may
as well recite the prayers for the dead for your friend. C.
Petronius Niger has him now. I am indeed very sorry."
And in truth, he obviously was.

Fortunately at that moment Philoxena was allowing
her face to be gently washed and a new gown to be
arranged upon her; she did not hear. Eugenius made the
Sign of the Snake, then began calculating what their
chances might be of drifting past Chiringium on the far
side of the river at night and without lights. Appledore
sat upon the coamings and shed some thin tears, for he
had grown fond of the younger man. And Augustus,
though he did not leave his own precious seat upon his
many precious bales, did at least express his deep regret
over the incident, and sighed that a fellow-caesar's
policy should be so unproductive.

And the day, meanwhile, was dying, dying, dying.

Peregrine sat long in thought. Then he went and
fetched the chart of the river. "Senator, your assistance, in this matter, would be—"

"Anything I can possibly offer in the way of information, my boy—"

Eugenius, too, was made of the council. He was
vehemently opposed to what Peregrine had in mind, but
by and by, and with many misgivings, he was persuaded to try it. "Yonder indeed lies the mouth of the

old channel," he said, pointing, "plugged as it is and has long been with all manner of sozzle and swamp. That great blasted oak marks its location, beyond which the rays of the setting sun are even now declining."

Peregrine nodded. "And now, Doctor Appledore," he said. *"If you please—"*

Once more, then, the strange harsh cry of the bird whose wings are spread wide upon the winds of the northern seas was heard. Faint, at first, and melancholy, as though the bird was idly skimming close to the waves, in search of something it knew not what, finding it not . . . then higher, and stronger, as if it had sighted what it sought, afar and off afar, and would reach it, and swiftly, too . . .

The breeze quickened in the darkling air. The breeze rose as the cry of the sea-bird rose, though no sea-bird was there seen, only Appledore, crouched upon the coamings, his cheeks beneath their colorless stubble all distended.

Peregrine felt that he was now not looking upon the faded landscape of a familiar-enough waterway inland in some temperate belt or clime. He seemed to see a wild waste of seas, far-off a region of savage rocks and snows. Fierce sprays filled the air. A single sea-bird rose upon the savage wind, rose higher, its cry rising.

—The sail cracked—once, twice, and a two times together, then—the sail filled with wind, the boat surged forward. Eugenius, his drawn face intent, steered his boat directly towards the shore . . . towards what seemed a stretch no different from any other stretch of shore, slightly to the right of the rearing skeleton of a blasted oak. The mast groaned, the sail strained, the ropes creaked their protest. The women huddled together, fearfully. Augustus had seemingly lost interest, and was perhaps trying (with the aid of a small pocket-abacus) to discover where, when, how

much. Senator Darlangius P. G. had a little book rather
suddenly in his right hand, from which he unhurriedly
read Psalms of Intercession; with his left hand he was,
perhaps absent-mindedly, caressing the ankle of
Philoxena.

The waters made a hissing sound as the boat raced
through them. Wild, wild, now, was the wind, and
fierce and hungry and strong. The sailing-barge went
into the land without a single pause—the land revealed,
then, instantly, as not true land at all; but, though
overgrown with grass and even thicketry, a water-
logged mass of mud and rotten tree-roots and sand and
water and weeds and reeds—driven by the might of the
wind, the *Homoiousios* cut through the *sudd* like a
knife through crusted porridge—the river, now unrestrained by the tangle which had long obscured its old
channel-mouth, and as well its waves driven by the
winds, broke through with a surge of mighty waters.

And on its crest, through the deepening darkness,
along the long-deserted as long-dry waterway, the boat
and all aboard of her went rushing onward.

Went rushing onward through the darkness.

Behind, where it was already dark, three domes of
broken wicker-work covered with tattered and filthy
felt, and settled somewhat lopsidedly on rough wagon-
beds, allowed their solid wheels to roll to a stop. The
few women and children settled down for the night
. . . or for however long it might be: these calculations
they left to their unlovely lords, and their unlovely lords
were off and away, far and away, on the gallop-a-trot.
*Keep the boat in sight,* had been their instructions, and
keep the boat in sight they would and were doing,
though to other eyes, perhaps, the boat and all things of
the daily word were now lost to sight, the eyes as the
ears of Hun Horde Number Seventeen were of other
quality and keenness. Day or night, land or water, trot

or swim, easy pace or hard, it was all one to any of them.

They placed their grubby great-toes a scruple more securely in the plaited-rope stirrups, and, as much at ease upon the boney backs of their sinewy little horses as any consul on his curule stool—in fact, considering the state of things in what was now the Central Roman Empire, more, much more—they floated and they followed on through the darkness. On and on and ever, ever on . . .

The arch-priest of the Church of San Stephanos had consulted his calendar and discovered that tonight was the Vigil of Saint Vespertilionid, a converted vampire of good family; and had, accordingly, with his deacon and his choir, set out to lead the small procession which was customary on such occasions. He had gone only a part of the way when he discovered that he was running low on incense. "Drat those pesky acolytes!" he exclaimed. "Well, there's no help for it, set a boy to do a man's job, if you want a thing done right do it yourself," he muttered; and sundry other saws and apothegms. "Well, well, Septimus," he said to his elderly deacon, "I'll just trot back and fill the incense-boat again; meanwhile, steady as you go for three more blocks and then turn left until you come to the dockside, and so on, and I'll meet up with you there, *tisk!*" and he scuttled back to his church as fast as he could. He was just as pleased, because the old supply of frankincense had come to an end, it was anyway (he considered) insufficiently smoky, and he was anxious to try out a new batch which he hoped would prove superior.

Deacon Septimus was on in years, and his ear was not what it was, and neither was his memory; instead of turning left as directed, he turned right. Until the last decade he had always turned right at this point anyway, for that way led the way to what for most of his long

lifetime had always been "the docks." It was all one to
most of the others, and those who were aware of the
mistake merely snickered and nudged each other.

"Silly old Sep has tooken the wrong turn!" they
whispered. "Old arch-priest, he won't half have the
wind up, as he find out, not half, hee hee!"

The elder who was languidly plonking the semantron
was a foreigner by birth and upbringing, whom some
long-forgotten upheaval in his native land of Egypt had
swept hither and deposited; he had not in all his years of
residence learned his way about the City, or much else
about it and its ways and customs.

Consequently, when the procession, followed with
varying degrees of interest or boredom by the invari-
able small throng of laymen, pietists and simple idlers,
reached the old docks; and reached them just in time to
observe that along the long-dry bed of the channel
rolled a rush of white-waved waters, bearing a ship
where no ship had been borne for many years, they
reacted in varying ways. The deacon somehow and
suddenly conceived the notion that something unusual
was happening, no doubt connected somehow with the
Vigil and the processions, and that he had forgotten
what this was. However, he would never in a million
years have admitted that his memory was failing. Instead, he lifted up his still-imposing voice and launched
into a *Te Deum*. The Egyptian elder, who had, in his
incredibly distant and unregenerative youth been a
worshipper of Isis, widened his rheumy eyes on behold-
ing what he assumed to be Isis Herself (it was actually
the Matron Eudoxia, clad in a garment from her native
Nubia, where Egyptian styles many years old were long
in going out of fashion) at the prow of the vessel. It was
evident to him that Isis had somehow been adapted into
the Church—an opinion which he had long been of
himself, to the cause of much difficulty at home long

ago—and now he paused not to reason as to details, but began to beat upon his far-sounding bell-board with might and main. The arch-priest arrived at just this moment, burdened with reproof at the wrong turning, but on observing something going on of which everyone but he seemed to be aware, he promptly stoked up the thurible with fresh incense and soon thick choking clouds of it were drifting all about, contributing nothing to the clarity of the scene and its events, but much to its air of mystery and authority.

The old channel just below the very end of the old dock had for some years now been used as a sort of public dump and into the vast and musty pile of rubbish the *Homoiousios* dug her nose so firmly that not all the long-pent and gurgling waters of the river could dislodge her. Aboard, Augustus the Penurious, seeing a crowd . . . a priest . . . a procession . . . hearing the same song which had been sung at his coronation . . . at once began to scrabble in his baggage for his purple and his crown. With a curt, "Well done, General," he handed these to Peregrine. "Hold these till ready—" and stepped ashore onto a group of pilings.

"My fellow-citizens," he began.

At these familiar words, lending for the first time an element of the understandable to the scene, the crowd let out a cheer. At the equally familiar, "O Senate and People of Rome!" they cheered again—particularly as they recognized aboard the familiar and friendly figure of P.C.D.B. Darlangius P. G., president of their Senate; who waved a hand at them, which held a wine-cup.

"I am pleased at your welcome of your new Caesar," continued Augustus, "and as you are here to hear what I have to say about my deep interest in your welfare, I shall lose no time in telling them to you. Take whatever work Providence or the Authorities—same

thing, same thing—are pleased to place you in, work
hard and productively, spend less than you earn, save
your money, never invest more than twenty percent in
any one thing, pay your taxes promptly, go to church
three times a day and after meals, visit only
government-inspected and -licensed brothels, avoid
heresy and other damnable doctrines, and thus you will
find true happiness—''

The crowd cheered lustily and then began a chant of,
*''Toss it off! Toss it off!''*

Few phrases could have been more immediately understandable to Augustus the Penurious, and he un-
stoppled the strings of his nearest moneybags: but he
was, after all, not called Stingy Gus for nothing: and a
strange and perhaps involuntary shyness or paralysis
took hold of him at this moment. In his ear he heard the
friendly Senator murmur, ''Don't stop *now*, for Pity's
sake!''—but he could not do otherwise than stop.

*''Toss it OFF! Toss it OFF!''* the cry continued,
and was now interspersed with a rhythmical clapping
sound. Still Gus stood there, with his hands plunged to
the wrists in bezants. With only a small sigh, then,
Senator D. set down his wine-cup and plunged his own
hands into the sagging sacks, and then, standing up,
began to toss the contents ashore with great and wide-
sweeping gestures. Six cohorts of troops arrived at this
moment, and, on seeing the traditional gesture, and one
which in their opinion had been insufficiently repeated
of recent years, they at once stacked spears and began
to elbow their way forward, pausing now and then to
scrabble with the rest.

Augustus lost part of his paralysis and began to howl
about his money. Peregrine said, ''Here you are, then,
sir. Imperial Scrip for the entire amount, redeemable at
any Bursary.''

''Straight down there to your left, past the public

micturarium,'' said the Senator, giving him a friendly pat. Augustus gestured, staggered, went down, still clutching the parchment, and was lost to sight. The Senator was interested in the entire pageant which was taking place in front of his eyes. Owing to the diligence with which he had been testing the ship's wine supplies, with a view to assuring himself of their wholesomeness, he found that he was not entirely sure what the nature of the pageant was. But he felt that it, like all pageants, was and must be a good thing. Only one thing vaguely troubled him at this moment, wrapped as he was in an aura of good wine and good will; and that was that there seemed to be a slight chill in the air.

''Boy, hand me my head-piece and my cloak,'' he said, absently to the figure at his elbow. This was Peregrine. To be involved in the civic and political affairs of Chiringirium was something he had not intended. It had in fact been his intention to by-pass the City afoot, as recommended. To C. Petronius Niger he had intended nothing whatsoever. But then came the capture of Claud, and there seemed no way to get him back from the hands of Black Pete save by prying loose the fingers of those hands. And so here they all were. His new friend was asking for something—

Peregrine blinked, cleared his throat, cupped his hands to his lips, and shouted, *''Ave! Ave! Ave! Ave . . . CAESAR!''*

Everyone stopped whatever he was doing, looked up and looked nervously around. And Peregrine, draping the purple robe around his friend's broad shoulders, and setting the diadem on his friend's head, announced in tones loud and clear and utterly assured, ''Proclaimed! Proclaimed is Publius Cato Decimus Brutus Darlangius Philipus Gordonius Caesar!''

Darlangius quite calmly reached up another fistful of bezants, tossed it in the direction of the most of the soldiers. And everyone shouted, "Hail Gordonius *Caesar!*"

The cohorts, having picked up what seemed to be the last of the bezants on the docks, knew well enough what the next step was. They stepped forward, placed their largest shield flat on the ground and hoisted the ample figure of the former President of the Senate on top of it; then they lifted it high. The throng cheered madly. The arch-priest turned and led the way back to the church in a thick and swirling cloud of incense, the choir singing happily and clutching their bezants. Darlangius Caesar bent slightly to one side, and said to Peregrine, "Well, my boy, it's six blocks to the scene of my anointing and investment, and it's six blocks the other way from Black Pete's palace. We either make it or we don't. Fortunately I have endowed several chantries and churches in the days of my richness, and also I've always made it a point to get all the pussy I could in hopes it would soak in. We'll see. We'll see."

It was at that point, frustrated in their attempts to follow the sailing-barge along her rapid route, and for the first time violating the letter of their orders, the fierce, feared, and wild hordesmen of Hun Horde Number Seventeen breached the walls of Chiringirium (via, it is true, the Dung Gate, which had been opened for the usual disposal of night-soil), and—with wild cries and hoots and shrill whistles, attacked.

That is, they went galloping down the street and, by singular coincidence, collided with the troops of Cnaeius Petronius Niger, alias Black Pete, who was rushing out of his palace to put down the commotion he did not fully understand in details but perfectly well in principle. The battle was brief.

Bloody, too.

"God-smoke," said Attila IV, wiping his knife on his left buttock, and sniffing the air with a practiced nose. "Jossee-men. Muchee gold clothes." His vexation at seeing the gold-clad priests accompanied by a caesar-figure who was himself accompanied by his ally Peregrine was swiftly tempered by the handfuls of tribute which both of them began ladling out to him. The Huns cast red eyes at the Christian matrons and maidens, but did not stop. Business, after all, was business.

"Don't forget to add, And *Conqueror of the Huns*, after *Defender of the Faith* and *Autarch and Autocrat*," said Darlangius Caesar. Then, something striking him at the same time it did Peregrine, he said, loud and clear, "Immediate release of all prisoners!" The congregation cheered. "Except, of course," the new ruler amended, "those up for adulterating wine!"

The congregation cheered again. And the choir sang *Amen* . . .

\*   \*   \*   \*

Darlangius was so pleased with the public pleasure at his accession to the purple that he announced that a General Anathema would be held at the Cathedral, with overflow services in the Hippodrome; and free refreshments at each. Now, there was nothing which more pleased the populace at that time more than a good General Anathema, allowing one to catch up with the latest theological info, as well as indulging in good old team spirit; and consequently the crowds were simply enormous. The archpriest of St. Stephanos, who had been elevated to archbishop, officiated. He was somewhat flustered, partly because he had never played the chief part in such a ceremony before, and partly because he had been firmly forbidden to employ the incense-burner in any capacity at all during the ceremony, by none other than Darlangius himself—"Reluctant though I should be to invoke the dubious doctrine of caesaropapism."

"Oh come on, don't be a beast, do!"

"Not a chance, No way."

"But my dear fellow I feel simply *lost* without my thurible—"

"If you get lost, I'll prompt you. Get on with it, now, the natives are getting restless."

The archbishop, with a desperate air of all-or-nothing (which, from the third row on back passed for an air of pronounced orthodoxy), arose and began the ceremony. Peregrine found it intensely interesting, if rather confusing. Where the archbishop knew his lines he ran through them at top speed in a sing-song tone, where he did not know them there was a good deal of muttering between him and the ever-helpful Caesar, and in between Peregrine could often clearly hear comments—not always *sotto voce*—from the congregation. The result was something as follows:

"Anathema maranatha be all heresies and heretics and may they be delivered unto Satan for the destruction of the flesh in order that the spirit may be saved and as Hymenaeus and Alexander were delivered unto Satan in order that they be taught not to blaspheme O factious of spirit be ye accursed and cast into eternal ruin and condemnation and afflicted with emmerods by the rod of the wrath of the Rord I mean Lord brfsk caff caff Cursed be they in coming in and cursed be they in going out cursed be they in rising up and cursed be they in lying down and in commerce and in consanguinity and prognostication and procrastination and in mint and anise and cumin and rue, allspice, almonds, assofoetida, butter or ghee, cardamoms, chillies, cinnamon, cloves, coconuts and their milk and oil, cream and whey, yak curds, yak turds, fenugreek, garlic, onions, ginger, lime, lime juice, vinegar, mace, mangoes, nutmegs, pepper, saffron, salt, tamarinds and turmeric—

". . . oh my i say no no no that seems to be, it is, a recipe for curry which i had of cosmo indicopleustes the doctrinally correct geographer, must have slipped in by mistake, you know how these things will happen, i wish i had my thurible"

". . . it sounds rather good"

". . . it *is* good, it is very good indeed, particularly with mutton, you know how mutton tends to be greasy"

". . . tends to be damned greasy, damn it, is the trouble with mutton"

". . . just so, well this cuts the grease, you know"

". . . i did no know"

". . . you most come and dine with us at the archpalace some day and we shall have it for tiffin"

". . . i say thanks very much i'd love to"

". . . delighted i'm sure"

The congregation, slightly mystified by this mumbling, received as it were enlightenment from an elderly girdflenser who announced, "Ah, they'm a-readin of the spicy bits up there, uh hur hur hur!"

The archbishop, hearing this, and being recalled to his duties, shuffled his vellums, and muttered:

". . . i can't find the place and i can't remember what is next, drat"

". . . vamp it, then, is what i always used to do in the senate when i was a bit buzzy: 'penitentiary and plenipotentiary' is one i always found useful"

"And cursed be they in penitentiary and plenipotentiary," gabbled the archbishop, still shuffling.

In the congregation: "That be some'at new" "Ur, and sound powerful strong" "What do it be for?" "Diddlin' thy niece" said the elderly girdflenser, who had a vigorous and singularly filthy imagination.

". . . and in weirdmane and womrath"

". . . adumbration, compurgation, obligation fenestration masturbation pro bono publico inter alia and in foro externo, fistula in ano, and e pluribus unam"

"Restitutia in integrum," chanted the archbishop.

*Congregation:* "Archbishop, he don't half give 'em Hell, do'e" "Serve they right, say I"

". . . i'm getting the hang of it, now, i think"

". . . doing just splendidly"

"Oh good here's the place, And may they mash their fingers with hammers—"

". . . something lost in translation there, i think"

". . . hush no one will know the difference—for inasmuch as they causeth enmities strifes jealousies wraths factions divisions envyings of the party of the first part and the party of the second part and other such damnable works of the flesh being proofs of a carnal mind and privily bim-bam," here the archbishop lost his place again, "dogs of the concision and grievous wolves not sparing the flock," finding it again, "seducing spirits and doctrines of devils first-class devils second-class devils and third-class devils (temporary) profane babblings and oppositions of the knowledge which is falsely so called," here he took a deep breath, "servants of Satan beasts in human form dealers in deadly poison robbers and pirates guilty of pride error disappointed ambition sensual lust avarice and pertinax defensio dogmatis ecclesiae universalis judicio condemnati in alphabetical order as follows:

"*Albigensians!*"

BOOM! went the big bass drum, just invented for the purpose, and thus making its first appearance on the stage of history.

"*Arians, Arminians, and Apollinarians!*"

BOOM! BOOM! BOOM!

*"Basilians!"* BOOM!

*"Cainites, Ebionites, and Gnostics!"* BOOM!
BOOM! BOOM!

*"Eutychesianites, Catharites, Hermaphrodites!"*

*Congregation:* "Ar, they'm be filthy boogers, they
morphadites"—BOOM! BOOM! BOOM!

Although the congregation were delighted out of
their gourds with the emphatic acoustical emphases of
the big bass drum, it plainly made the archbishop uneasy ("Jumped like a goosed twit," was the way
Caesar himself put it, later); and he began to run
through the list in a manner which made aged connois-
seurs of General Anathemas shake their venerable
heads and groan; lumping together Nestorians and Pre-
torians, Essenes and Manichees, Patrippassians, Sabel-
lians, Valentinians, Monarchianites and Monophysites, Pelagianists and Plagiarists.

"We brand them with infamy, condemn their con-
venticles, confround their politics, frustrate their
knavish tricks, oh my goodness, I forgot to include
Donatists and Monatists!"

BOOM! went the big bass drum. BOOM! And,
Caesar giving the signal, it continued to go BOOM!
BOOM! BOOM! until, finally, he taking pity on the
quaking prelate, gave him leave to swing the thurible.
As lagniappe he broke out a store of the rare No. 1
Jumbo Tribute Incense (Lebanon Red), and in short
order the thick, rich, reeking thunderheads began inex-
orably to send the crowds out of the cathedral and into
the refreshment tents; whilst the archbishop himself,
totally unaware that he was being abandoned, giggled
happily as he swung the burner and censed the invisible
and rapidly absquatulating congregation.

In the tents, by Decree, was spread out a lavish array
of pilchards, plovers, peacock, poppycock, plumduff,

pistachio nuts, pulse, and pease-porridge-hot, pease-porridge-cold—but not, at which there were some grumbles, not pease-porridge-in-the-pot-nine-days-old; Caesar not having known nine days before that he was going to find himself in the position of Chief Caterer of Chiringirium.

"Eat up, everybody," he urged, walking to and fro: "cost me a fortune."

"Will you be able to pay for it?" asked Peregrine, not seeing in Darlangius the same sort of single-minded fiscality which had characterized, let us say, Stingy Gus.

"Oh yes," the new ruler said, easily. "Secret Police Fund takes care of all that."

Peregrine thought this over for a moment, then was moved to ask what the police had to do with it.

"That's the secret."

Also present, and moving rather gingerly, was Claud; and now and then he rubbed his wrists and his elbows and felt about his throat, as though for reassurance. The eye of Darlangius fell upon him, and he beckoned. "Young man," he said, "not only do I feel that the State owes you a recompense, but I am fully aware that, had it not been for your imprisonment, *I* should now be still in the ranks of the penniless laity, a state from which I am grateful that Providence was pleased to remove me. Now, I am going to offer *all* of you boys cushy jobs. But *you*, my dear Clot—what did you say your—oh, Claud—you get first pick. How would you like to be Grand Logothete, say, or Lord Privy Part? *No?* I hope that you are not thinking of getting a transfer into your present position as Chief Scout?—because in my opinion you are a *lousy* scout. I don't think you could find elephant tracks in the snow."

Claud grimaced, looked rueful. "Well, be that as it

may," he said, "I sure have learned a lot about the horses in the hinterland of this province. I must know the pedigree and the good and bad points of every single one."

Caesar raised his eyebrows. "Is that so? Well, in that case, how about being the Chief Purchasing Agent, Cavalry?" Claud thought it over, exchanged looks with Philoxena, then turned back and nodded. "Excellent," said Caesar. "Try some of this lamprey-*mayonnaise*, it's delicious."

Peregrine said, "What? . . . Claud? . . . You're leaving us?"

"What, 'leaving us?' "

"I mean, you're not coming along with us?"

"Coming along *where?*" demanded Claud, a trifle testily. "I am content to stay, I hope you'll stay, but if you *don't* stay, then it seems to me that it's *you* who's 'leaving us,' if you see what I mean."

Peregrine thought it all over. Claud was giving up a place as companion? thrall? to a gentleman-adventurer? wandering bastard? and was taking instead a job in the Imperial Civil Service which was of such a nature that it would endure through untold reigns and upheavals (not that there were any signs of such here): one which must pay well and which carried with it a certain fixed position in the social scale—if not the very highest, certainly not the very lowest. Not for him to seek an all-but-unknown princess when he already had a woman who was sincerely devoted to him. Where Austin, son of Palindrome, might be, was of only minimal and academic interest to Claudius, son of who? And as for baleful beechen boards, he was as innocent as a babe unborn. And so Peregrine concluded that he did indeed see what Claud meant.

By unspoken command, then, Claud and Peregrine and Caesar Augustus (sipping from a gemmed goblet filled with a rare vintage laid down in days long gone by a hedonistic predecessor with a nice palate himself) turned to Appledore. The latter had bellied up to the enormous silver salad-bowl containing the lamprey-*mayonnaise* as though it were going to be included any minute now in another General Anathema. After a moment he observed that they were waiting for his answer, and he wiped his mouth on a square of fine linen (embroidered *et ux Mesilissa*, it had perhaps once or twice been put to other purposes).

"Well, I'll tell you, my boy—my boys—and Caesar—it all depends. I should wish first to get together with my old schoolmate, the philosopher Volumnius, and talk things over. And I'd have to meditate the matter. So . . . as of right now . . . I don't know . . . ." And he returned to his salad.

"There," said Caesar, "you see? What's your hurry? Hot pants? What's out there that isn't here, and of better quality, too? Take it easy. Stick around. Have another drink. Take in the ceremony. There's a pretty pageant coming up. I disband the standing army with severance pay and passports—hint, hint—and create local militias: The Army of the First Ward, South, and so on. Bishops bless the banners. Then we install the new rank which I have created. This one is practically a beauty contest. Majorettes of the Drum. Some of the boobs on these broads would knock your helmet off."

Interested in spite of his uncertainties, Peregrine asked, "And who is going to judge the beauty contest?"

Caesar gave him the smile of a man in full fig and vigour who has just fully realized the implications of the *jus primae noctis*, and, teetering up and down on his feet and rubbing his hands together, (very softly), "Caesar," he said.

# PART
# 5

By abolishing the dreaded secret police, of which the late caesar C. Petronius Niger, had made wide use, Darlangius at one stroke was made free of enough funds on hand to pay for all sorts of public benefits without having to raise taxes by a penny. He repaired the aqueducts, re-opened the baths, dedicated three new cathedrals (each, of course, named Hagia Sophia), repaired the walls, and for one entire week had the public supply of fountains run with wine from five to six in the evening. There were also, needless to say, games and processions and beauty contests galore. Indeed, no caesar had ever been so wildly and so widely popular as this one; and when a certain tax-farmer, one Macromius, was heard to mutter that the new autarch and autocrat was "nothing but a fat fornicator," he was pelted with offals by indignant market-women. And hot and cold collations were laid on at the Domicile, so that Peregrine for the first time was able to see, smell, taste, touch, and—had he desired—wallow in such dainties as breaded kids' kidneys and suckling pigs with truffles in their noses.

However, although it would be of all possible exaggerations the greatest to say that to a young man of healthy appetites, even the joys of breaded kids' kidneys, of suckling pigs with truffles in their noses (to say nothing of judging beauty contests and then taking the winners out for a little wine and frolic), could pall —still . . . still . . . something seemed to gnaw and to nibble on the periphery of Peregrine's mind.

He found Darlangius engaged with his Chief Herald

in the task of drawing up coats of arms for the Sanitary
Disposal Corps, and evidently not pleased with the
sample in hand. "A swine sejant on a mess—I suppose
that's meant to be fess, but mess would be better—take
it away, I've never seen such bumtwaddle in my life.
Look here, simply incorporate them as the Guild of
Saint, oh, Saint . . . well, ask my chaplain to pick a
nice vacant saint, and have him painted on the biggest
banner they can carry: Guild of Saint Vacantsaint.
Patron: HH The Caesar. And twice a year they can
carry it in procession, and after that there'll be a bean-
feast, paid for out of the garbage rates. —Ah, Peregrine, my young friend! Draw up a curule stool.
—Very well, Bumpus, that will be all.''

(It was, however, not quite all. Bumpus, who was
simply not with it save in his niche as Chief Herald,
stolidly went and informed the Chaplain of the
Domicile that HH wanted prepared a big banner of
Saint Vacantsaint; the chaplain, a distant and poor
relation, who had already been twice unfrocked
—once, for clandestine nose-picking during Lent, and
once for open and notorious omphiloskepsis—and had
not fully realized his present good fortune and security,
promptly went into a dither. It was (he felt) out of the
question to admit that he had never heard of any Saint
Vacantsaint. So he retrieved an image which had been
so badly disfigured during the Iconoclastic outrages
that no one really knew whose it was, and turned it over
to the banner-painter to be used as a model. The
banner-painter operated on the serene and simple principle of, Whatever is, is right—or, Don't rock the boat.
He painted the saint large, but he painted him as he saw
him, to wit: without a nose. And wit was soon to find an
explanation, namely that this was so much the better,
for thus Saint was unable to smell the muck-carts. The
muck-men were men of a robust, not to say coarse,

humor, and this pleased them mightily. "That 'ere noo Caesar, 'e do be a caution!" they guffawed. "So much the better as Saint Vacantsaint 'ave no nose, for so 'e can't smell they muck-carts, har har har!" Legend promptly revealed that the saint had lost this member at the hands of a wicked pagan emperor, and in no time at all he was curing piles, scabies, bad dreams, trench-mouth, the common cold, crossed conditions, husband-come-home, and—inevitably, and perhaps with some slight assistance from a vigorous choir-boy—barrenness. A century later, chroniclers were still writing, in uncials and miniscules, *But in ye days of Darlangius Cye Faith flourishd.)*

"What's on your mind, my boy? You getting much?"

"Oh, I get enough . . ."

"Nonsense. No man ever gets enough. There's either not enough or there's too much, and the last man who had too much died sometime before Caligula's horse. —Not, I hasten to imply, that I mean to imply anything against any of my predecessors in the consu-late. There was nothing queer about Caligula's horse."

"Well, I—"

"*Nothing* queer about him. Probably performed his consular duties as well as many, too. As for his master, my august ancestor under the principle of spiritual consanguinity, well, he and Black Pete probably have a lot to talk over together on the Stygian Riviera. Come, come, speak up, I'm a rich, busy man," he declared, lying back on his couch, and nibbling rapidly at a bunch of grapes. "What's on your mind?"

Peregrine said, somewhat slowly, that he was won-dering about the "young woman of good family" at whose home the soldiers of Petronius Niger came look-ing for Austin. "Do you suppose," he suggested, "that she might have some idea as to where he went? . . ."

"He went out the backway and over the wall, is all *I* know. But then, hm, you didn't ask if *I* had any idea, you asked if *she* might. I don't know. Why don't you ask *her?*"

"Well, for one thing, I don't know who she is. Or where she lives. Or—"

"That will do, that will do. Stop, before you make things harder. Well, her name is Clothilda, and she lives on the Flaminian Way, and—"

"What, in *Rome?*"

"No, not in Rome. Drink deeply, or touch not the Pierian spring—I found that in a fortune cooky once—*every* provincial capital has its Flaminian Way, just as it has its Hippodrome, its Pantheon—formerly devoted to the worship of abominations—, and so on. *This* Flaminian Way used to be the most fashionable residential area in town, but that was before the Christians started moving into it. However, there are still a number of nicely kept-up villas there.

"And one of the nicest is that of T. Pomponius Sulla. Tell him I sent you."

The name rang no semantrons in Peregrine's mind. "T. Pomponius Sulla," he said, blankly. "Who is he?"

Said Caesar, "He's Clothilda's husband."

*    *    *    *

The Villa Sulla had not been subdivided to make room for the multitudes of countrypeople who were still swarming into the cities of the Central Roman Empire as life in the rurals became daily more hazardous; unlike many of the other properties, then, even as Caesar had hinted, on the Flaminian Way, it had not become a human rabbit-warren. Its trim lawn and

clipped hedges testified to the existence of a staff as
silent and semi-invisible as they were efficient. It was
perhaps as the result of the changing neighborhood that
the walls surrounding this area of grace and opulence
were pierced on the street side only by a single door,
and that at Peregrine's knock this door did not swing
open: but another and very tiny door did open in the
upper part of the greater, and through this small aper-
ture an eye regarded him without blinking.

"Caesar sent me," said Peregrine.

T. Pomponius Sulla, despite his very Roman-
sounding name, very apparently originated under a
much hotter sun than that which shines on Father
Tiber's shores . . . to say nothing of shores farther
north. Without regard to current fashion, he was
smooth-shaven, and his almost white hair was clipped
very close to his head. Head and shoulders were bent,
as Peregrine approached, though neither this nor the
whiteness of the host's hair seemed in any way to
indicate great age. To one side of the marble bench in
the garden on which Sulla was sitting a lector stood
with a scroll open in his hands, reading aloud.

> *Death at the headland, Hesiod, long ago*
> *Gave thee to drink of his unhoneyed wine.*
> *Now Boreas cannot harm thee, flying low—*

Sulla raised his head and his hand, and the lector
ceased as though sheared off with a scissors. Dark,
glowing eyes regarded Peregrine with an enigmatic
calm, and, as the young man gazed at and into them, he
perceived that they were after all not so dark as he had
thought, being nearer to yellow than to brown, and
flecked with gold, which seemed slowly to shift and
drift. T. Pomponius Sulla raised a hand again, and at

once, as though waiting all the while, a chair appeared
. . . and a small table . . . wine . . . water . . . a
mixing bowl . . . a goblet was gently placed in
Peregrine's hands.

"Welcome, sir . . . I think that I do not say,
*Citizen?*"

Peregrine nodded. "That is to say, not that you are
not of rank to be a citizen," a faint, polite smile briefly
acknowledged the absurdity of this possibility, vanished at once, "but that you are, I believe, that rather
*rara avis*, a foreigner who is not a barbarian." Sulla's
own Latin was more than flawless, it was beautiful, and
seemed enriched, now and then, with traces of another
accent . . . Punic, perhaps? or Numidian? . . . which
Peregrine, with his limited experience and knowledge,
could not identify. He thought vaguely of this, and
vaguely of other things, and was vaguely aware that his
host's eyes had gone past him and were looking at his
hands, or, rather at what his hands were doing, or had
only just done. And then he went a trifle cold, as he
realized that without thinking he had done something
which he had not done in some while: he had poured a
libation.

"Ah," said Sulla, softly. "You are a pagan. Or," he
went on, tactfully, and without pause, "you have been
one." He made no further reference to the gesture.
Peregrine, who had tensed, relaxed. He realized that it
had, after all, been about a pagan poet which Sulla's
lector had been reading; and not a Father of the Church,
or a Martyr. Nor were there any evidences of Christian-
ity visible—no ikons, no crosses. But, his host saying
nothing, he said nothing himself.

"So Caesar sent you . . . . That was kind of him."

"The kindness, sir, was to me."

"No. Caesar knows of my continued interest in the
world beyond the City's walls, although I myself have

not passed beyond those walls in some time . . . . For that matter, it has been some time since I have even passed beyond the walls of the Villa Sulla. Nevertheless. Yes. Generally speaking, I hold aloof from making much observance or taking much notice of changes in administration, they being generally for the worse, one Co-Heir of the Emperor succeeding another Co-Heir in rather rough and rapid fashion . . . Indeed, as one hears, once Emperor succeeds another nowadays. It is small wonder that the Emperors take little or no notice of the multitude of Conjoint Sebastocrators who supposedly stand ready to succeed them. I myself am not even precisely sure at present who it is that occupies the Throne in Ravenna—or, for that matter, Rome—or Byzantium. However, in this instance the change is certainly for the better, for Darlangius is not inherently vicious.''

Peregrine regarded this as one of the faintest and most qualified compliments which he had heard in a long time. Sulla passed easily enough from that subject to others, asking polite questions to which Peregrine for the most part answered equally easily; and, when he could not, the host changed the subject in such a manner as to avoid embarrassment to him. And so by and by he heard Sulla enquire, ''And shall you, then, remain here? In Chiringirium?''

As Peregrine did not feel that he could give the truthful answer, which would have been phrased somewhat as, ''Well, that depends on what I may or may not hear from your wife, who is really the one I came to see; so how about it?'' He did the next best he could, and said that he was not certain, he thought that he would not stay, but he was not certain when he would go if he did go.

Sulla nodded. ''Young men tend not to settle. They tend to be impetuous, of a sanguine humor is how, I

believe, Science puts it. I hope that you will be my
guest for dinner—'' At this Peregrine's heart gave a
little leap "—not, of course, tonight," Sulla swept on,
smoothly, "for you will naturally have made other
arrangements. But in a day or two I shall send you an
invitation, in enough time for you to include it in your
inevitably rather busy schedule. I quite understand that
you are not able to stay longer with us today, and, much
though I should wish to, must not attempt to delay
you." As he was saying this, Sulla was rising, and,
Peregrine not entirely knowing just how it was happening, saw nothing for it but to say farewell to his host,
and to follow the silent servitor who was bowing before
him.

They passed through two courts as they had entered
and then, seeing gardeners spraying with wide gestures
an area which lay ahead of them at some distance, the
servitor murmured an apology, and they turned and
proceeded by a second route.

This took them through a part of the villa itself, and
Peregrine observed that, richly-furnished though it
was, it was not in any degree over-furnished. And then
she was there, and when he turned, automatically,
though not exactly knowing why, to his guide, he
realized, suddenly, that no one else was there but they
two.

Peregrine had thought that she might be big and
blonde, only later realizing that he thought this only
because his brother himself was big and blonde; or—he
had thought—she might be dark and opulent; and this,
he subsequently perceived, was only because he had
discerned in himself, recently, such a taste. She was,
however, dark and slight. Not even slender. Slight. No
one would have said that she was beautiful, as no one
would have said that she was ugly. And, certainly,

*plain*, gods knew, in no way began to describe her. She was, then, Clothilda, and she was herself.

"Have you news? —You are very much like him," she said. Eagerness to hear gave way to a desire to put Peregrine at his ease, and, in a moment—no more—she had done so. He soon told her of the only two pieces of information he had found of Austin during his travels so far—that he had passed through a misty and mysterious mountain region, and, thence, had gone by a route which went "right over left, left over right"—and that, eventually thereafter, he had come to Chiringirium— "As have you," she said. "And I am very glad." Then, at once, it was easy for him to speak and they spoke together, intermingling words and information: how, Austin, as a small boy . . . how, Austin, a grown man, and here . . . what he was like then and now . . . what he was not like, now as then . . .

"But have you an idea where he went?" demanded Peregrine.

Her face lost its laughter-lines. "I do not know," she said, low-voiced. "I do not know . . ."

"Perhaps you *may* know, though," he persisted; "you may be knowing without knowing that you know . . . you know?" Despite herself, she did laugh at this. He explained, as best he could, that it may have been that his brother Austin could have mentioned some place which he would want to visit . . . would want to see . . . had, at least, expressed interest in . . . Or, conversely, had spoken of an area, a province, a country, a climate—even—which he thought not well of, would never want to see. "Now. You do see what I mean, yes? So now, what think you, lady Clothilda?"

She nodded, seriously. She sighed, soft. Her slight fingers drummed upon the small table in front of her. "Peregrine, listen . . . Tonight I shall dedicate to

thinking of this. I shall put aside other thoughts and I
shall lie with my lamps lit and my tablets in one hand
and my stylus in the other. And I shall think of Austin,
only of Austin, and I shall bring him back, in my own
thoughts—oh, not dreaming dreams of him, no—but
striving to recall every word he said, and even the
expression on his face when, perhaps, someone else
said certain words. And each possibility as it occurs to
me, I shall write it down. And I shall be in touch with
you . . . Younger Brother . . ."

The same silent servitor seemed to materialize and to
guide Peregrine out of the Villa Sulla, and Peregrine at
first did not, could not, identify the squawk of surprise
and of so much more than surprise as coming from that
silent mouth: the same instant something like an
enormous cobweb obscured his sight, fell in heavy
folds upon his shoulders and his limbs, tripped his feet
and tangled his hands . . . He fell painfully, ropes
jerked tightly, were gathered tautly. He floundered,
was turned over, trussed like a calf for market. A figure
stood in front of him as he was jerked to his feet.

With some half-formed notion of bravado, and
more—a great deal more—than half-confused, Peregrine said, "Is that a reticularis which I see before me?
If so, where is your trident?"

His words were ignored. For a long, long moment
the figure looked at him in silence. The gold-flecked
eyes burned into his own; there were no whites around
them now, only red. Red, red flecks burned among the
gold. The servitor, trussed, himself, like a pigeon, gave
one more squawk. Was kicked, swiftly, skillfully.
Retched, dryly, fell, was silent. "That one," said
Sulla, "I shall certainly and presently crucify."

"So," he said. "The sons of Sapodilla. Are there
perhaps more of you? Was one not enough, and more
than enough? Did you perhaps think that I had taken her

to be my wife and kept her as such, staying here as I have done and as I thought guarding her for her sake, in order that the bastard sons of some brute hill chief might slip in again and again to tread her like a dunghill hen is trodden? O dunghill cocks'' his voice stopped without breaking or even rising or falling. For some slow second he had clearly ceased to breathe. Then his breath came and it caught in his breast. He struggled, conquered. In the same level tone: ''That one I shall certainly and presently crucify,'' he said. ''But as for you, though you were Caesar's son and Born-in-the-Purple, yet I do swear that no such easy and rapid death should be yours.—*Take!*''

\*   \*   \*   \*

Tradition demanded that the way into a dungeon be led by guttering torches: T. Pomponius Sulla, however traditionally-minded he might be on other matters, was not concerned with this aspect of it. The way was led by a somewhat stout butler carrying an enormous tray partly balanced on his paunch, and the tray was crowded with small and conventional terra-cotta oil-lamps, all lit. Whenever they came to a niche bearing a burned-out lamp, the butler deftly whisked a fresh one into its place and put the empty on the tray.

The party paused at one place while the master of the villa took up a lamp and held it into a side-chamber filled with amphorae. ''Is that the falernian from the year of the Consulate of L. Tiberius Nerva?'' he asked.

''Yes, Sir T.,'' the butler said.

''You may as well start decanting some of it for the table, tomorrow, Sempronius.''

''Very good, Sir T.''

''We shan't be able to get any more of it, you know.''

"Alas, no, Sir T."

"And if you catch any of the kitchen-boys sipping it, dip their fingers in hot oil, do you hear?"

"Yes, Sir T. Very good, Sir T."

They started off again, occasionally treading on ugly white patches of fungus. Ichor dripped greenly from the clammy walls in places. In another, three skeletons in armor dangled from chains. T. Pomponius Sulla clicked his tongue. "I thought we had gotten rid of those," he said, in annoyance.

"Such were Your Honor's orders, Sir T.," said Sempronius. "But the blacksmith has been suffering severely from swollen joints and finds it impossible to remain in the crypt long enough to remove the shackles."

"Well, well," muttered the master of the Villa Sulla, "then we must simply wait till he is feeling better, poor old chap. As Epictetus puts it, There are things which can be helped and there are things which cannot be helped. Eh?"

"Exactly so, Sir T."

T. Pomponius Sulla gave a sigh. Then he stopped and gestured with the hand holding the lamp, casting great leaping shadows. "How about this one?" he asked. "Who's in there?"

The butler consulted his little list, having first carefully set down the tray of lamps upon a pile of skulls. "In this one, Your Honor, is the philosopher Volumnius, who, after a dinner of farced nightingales and unmindful both of the duties of a guest and of Your Honor's vastly superior knowledge of such, as of all, subjects, had the temerity to dispute Your Honor's judgements on the *oktosyllable* and the *dekasyllable*—"

"Ah yes. I remember now. Nobody can say that I am not a reasonable person, but it's a funny thing about

me, Sempronius. If there's one thing I can't stand, it's
being contradicted. Ah well. *Errare humanum est*, you
in there, do you recant?''

After a moment a weak, hollow voice was heard to
say, ''It does not lie within my power to disobey, but
neither am I obliged to comply. I may be constrained. I
am constrained? Very well, then, I am constrained. Is it
just that I be constrained? Is it, for that matter, just that
my nose run? Better to wipe it than to complain. There
is a place in poetry for the *oktosyllable* and there is a
place in poetry for the *dekasyllable* and when the one is
used where it is meet that the other is used, the result is
not poetry, it is chaos. According to *The Enclitics of
Euphrastus*, Book XXIII, versicle—''

But T. Pomponius Sulla, with an oath, had ceased to
cup his ears against the echoes. ''Damn the fellow,
well, there you are, that's what it is to start up with one
of those damned philosophers. —Stay there, then!'' he
shouted. And turning to his servants, he ordered, with
another gesture, ''String him up!'' and, in a trice,
Peregrine found himself simultaneously free of the net
and with his left leg in fetters.

''Lace up the right one, too.''

''The bolt seems to be missing, Your Honor.''

His Honor sighed the sigh of the long-suffering.
''Must I see to everything?'' he asked, rhetorically. He
clicked his tongue and retreated with one of the only
two remaining lit lamps to a far corner of the next
chamber. In the dimness Peregrine, staring at his fet-
tered foot, was astonished to see another foot, gaunt
and filthy and definitely not his, come out of the darkness and, seizing a rope's end between the great- and
the adjacent toe, whip it back and out of sight with an
audible snap. ''What was that?'' demanded T. Pomponius, suddenly appearing with the other lamp.

''Rats, Your Honor.''

"Ah. Good. —Sempronius. Look here." Lord, servants, lamp, vanished again. From the darkness came a screech, a groan, and a frightful wail of agony, such as set Peregrine's smaller hairs upright, and all his teeth on edge.

"There. You see? The damned rack is simply a mass of rust! How am I supposed to torture anyone when the rack is simply a damned mass of rust? Is there no neat's-foot oil?"

"There should certainly be neat's-foot oil in the buttery, Sir T."

"You mean, unless the buttery-thralls have been dressing their salad with it again." Sempronius made a noncommittal noise.

"Well, see to it, and if there isn't any, torture the thralls and send down to the shops for some more . . . . Let me see. Something else on my mind. What was it?"

There was a pause, evidently long enough for Sempronius to consult his list once more. "Your Honor was going to crucify the servitor Julianus."

"Oh yes. Yes. I was, wasn't I? That's the filthy traitor we left lashed up in the forward hole, isn't it? Do it directly. No, I won't, either. Not enough time. Must dine with my wife. Lovely woman. Weak, of course. But there you are. Women, you know. Weak. Well, well, let's get on with it, or the blacksmith won't be the only one suffering from swollen joints. Dreadful chill and damp down here, don't know why the government allows it."

The shadows cast by the other lamp stretched out into infinity, faded away along with the footsteps, and the echoes of the voice of T. Pomponius Sulla, muttering, "Weak, weak, weak, weak, weak, weak, weak, weak, weak, weak, weak, weak," until at length dying away into a whisper. Distant and damnably thick doors clanged shut.

And at last there was silence.

"Well, at least they forgot the lamp," said a rather rusty-sounding voice.

"Oh, good," said Peregrine. "Then I can read myself to sleep."

Something like a chuckle came from the shadows. "No, don't do that," said the voice. "Bad for your eyes. —Well," it went on, "you have seen at least one facet of the complex psyche which constitutes T. Pomponius Sulla; how do you like it?"

Peregrine said that he had seen at least three facets of the complex psyche which constituted T. Pomponius Sulla, and he asked how many there were. A considering mumble terminated in the conjecture that there were probably at least three hundred. "Well, I'm sure I won't like any of them," the young man said.

"What are you in for?"

"For supposedly betraying Sulla with his wife, the lady Clothilda."

"And did you?"

"Certainly not!"

A tongue was clicked. "Your tone, my fellow-prisoner, seems to be one of indignation at my question, instead of which it should be one of great regret. You are, after all, receiving the punishment anyway. Why, therefore, should you not have committed the crime?"

Peregrine thought this over, and realized, to his mild surprise, that the indignation was not at the suggestion that he might have betrayed Sulla but at the implication that he might have betrayed Austin. And on this he meditated for a further while, until he was interrupted by the sight of Volumnius retrieving the filched rope from the shadows and commencing to coil it up neatly with some slight murmur of gratification. "That *was* neatly done," he observed.

"Thank you. I think it was, rather."

"And what do you intend to do with it?"

"Do with it? Well, I hadn't exactly planned what to do with it. I don't think it would become me, as a Philosopher, to be over-concerned with the immediately practical aspects of things. Life is not merely for the moment. And, even if I am not able to utilize it, perhaps there may come one or more after me, to whom it may prove utile."

The implications of these words were somewhat slow in sinking into Peregrine's mind, but when they did, he shuddered. After a moment, swallowing a large and awkward Nothing which had lodged in his throat, he said, rather tentatively, "Uh . . . do they, uh . . . *feed* us here?"

The philosopher looked up in some surprise. "Certainly they feed us," he said. "They *must*. It's the law, you know. All persons keeping prisoners in private dungeons and/or crypts must supply them with a ration consisting in not less than one half of a quarter loaf per diem, delivered not less often than every third day; plus, once every third day, a piece of salt junk not smaller than a small man's hand; *plus* water, quantity sufficient to drown a large rat."

"Also," he added, after a moment, "during Lent and Fast Days, either cheese or a double quantity of pulse is substituted for the salt junk."

Peregrine thought this over, too; and asked if it was customary to drown the large rat each time in order to be sure that the water was of the requisite amount. Volumnius shrugged. One usually placed, he said, a small piece of food in the basin in order to tempt the rats, who thus generally drowned themselves. This was done, not to test the legality of the liquid rations, but in order to supplement the rations.

"I hope you dined well before being seized, because it's two more days till feeding time. —What? Not hungry? Well, if you *get* hungry, let me know, I have some nice rat which is more or less pickled in a brine derived from soaking salt junk. Eh? The very thought gags you, does it? Hoity-toity. 'Tis easy to see that *you* are no philosopher. Well, well. Mustn't brood, you know. Here. Let me entertain you. Shall I show you my shop? Did you know that I keep a shop here?"

And with no more than an occasional dotty cackle, the philosopher proceeded to show him all sorts of things which he had squirreled away over in his corner of the darkness; such as large and small amphorae, dried bread, grated cheese, pickled rat, pieces of scrap metal including an old sun-dial, old clothes, old chains and fetters, instruments of torture, pieces of wood, and sundry segments and specimens of this and that; all of which would not have seemed out of place in the establishment of Ulrich, who sold broken swords by weight. "Passes the time," explained the philosopher, with a shrug. "What'll you buy? What'll you buy?" he chanted, imitating the shopkeeper's cry.

"I used to keep a blacksmith's shop," he explained, "but I brought it back." He then disclosed some bits of papyrus and a number of old keys, and was rummaging in the niches and caches of his corner when something scratched at Peregrine's mind.

"What do you mean, you brought it back?"

"I mean that I used to occupy myself by pretending to use the smithy-implements and so on. But one day I was asleep when they came down and awoke in bare time to restore the things to their place over yonder. After that I let them alone."

Peregrine thought this over carefully. He was not

entirely sure of what it might mean. "*That* sounds like a more interesting game!" he said, "Much more so than mere shopkeeping."

"Do you really think so? Sure? Well, well, *de gustibus*," and, with a slight shrug, Volumnius calmly reached up and gave his chain a tug. The ring-bolt popped out of its rusty hole in the dungeon wall and Volumnius, neatly wrapping his chains about him as though they were the folds of a toga, walked out of the doorless cell and into the next chamber. And, from thence, he returned, bearing hammer and chisels and bellows. "Who'll be the horsey?" he asked. "Do you want to be the horsey?"

"Can't shoe the horsey without a fire to bend the horsey-shoes!" Peregrine said, merrily.

"One fire, coming up!"

Clanking cheerfully, Volumnius trotted back with brazier and charcoals. Peregrine, who had, needless to say, already tested his own chain and ringbolt, now began to build up a fire-base of old papyrus and scraps of wood. Then he reached out and took fire from the lamp with a wisp of old rope. At once his fellow-prisoner raised a cry of alarm.

"But you are not really going to *light* the fire—*are* you?"

"Of course I am," Peregrine said, doing so. "Why not?"

"Well, for one thing, the fumes of charcoal are deadly poisonous—"

"In an enclosed and airless place, certainly. In this enormous crypt, certainly not."

"And furthermore, if they find upon their next return what we have been up to, they will be simply furious!"

Peregrine muttered something about crossing that bridge when he came to it. He broke off small bits of charcoal, just as he had often seen done at his father's stable-forge, and gradually built up a small fire. Volumnius, torn between pleasure and apprehension, made an uncertain movement towards the bellows. "Not yet," said Peregrine. "Perhaps you have a fan . . . er . . . shopkeeper?"

"Certainly I have a fan!" said the older man, at once falling happily into the game once more. "Best quality Egyptian ware, and the very latest fashion in Ravenna," he said, holding up a filthy but still serviceable item.

"I'll take it."

"That will be eight drachmas, please."

"Put it on my bill."

"Sorry, ours is a strictly one-price, cash-and-carry establishment."

"Volumnius," Peregrine said, quietly, "fan the fire or I'll brain you with this hammer."

"Oh, very *well*," said the philosopher, rather sulkily. "But where's your sense of *fun?*"

The anvil, of course, could not be moved, but a fairly large and fairly flat stone was wedged up from the far corner and rolled near enough to serve. It took a while for the fire, now at last rushed on with bellows, to grow hot enough; and longer, for that part of Peregrine's chain (as near to the ankle as he could manage) to grow red and soft. Frequently he changed the sopping-wet rags which protected him from the fire's heat and limited the heat from extending too much from the links in the forge along with the rest of the chain and to the fetters and finally to his flesh. But, at long enough last, he was able to strike well enough with hammer and chisel to sever the chain.

"Shopkeeper, have you by any chance more oil?"

"Yes, yes, let me see where did I oh in this old jar

here, first pressing of the vine, prime quality—Fill the lamp? Certainly sir. And that will be . . ." Here he glanced again at the hammer, said, "I'll put that on your bill, shall I sir? . . ."

The servitor Julianus was so quiet, back in the forward hole, that Peregrine thought he was dead. But the eyes moved slowly and fearfully in the light of the dim and flaring lamp. And when Peregrine placed his hand on the man's shoulder, meaning no more than a gesture of reassurance, he moaned and seemed to fall away, somehow, to fall away and to shrink in upon himself: and his flesh was cold.

"Here, now, man, take heed," Peregrine said, dismayed. "Don't you see that I am not your half-mad master, but your fellow-prisoner?" Julianus perhaps perceived some little, at least, of this; for now his eyes ceased to rest upon them, but were fixed in the direction along which death would come. "Enough of talking, to work," Peregrine said. He tested the bolt in the wall, but it was firm. By greater good fortune than poor Julianus was then capable of grasping, however, several of the links were almost half-rusted through. There was no need to go back and move the forge-gear in its entirety. A hundred blows, more or less, with the cold-chisel, sufficed to part them. Julianus took one step, took two, fell forward.

Peregrine reached out to uphold him, but the man eluded his grasp, fell to his knees, and kissed Peregrine's feet. Then he raised his head, and embracing the knees of the man who had freed him, said, "I am your liege man of love and of loyalty and of all homage and all honor, of all duty, even unto death, from now and forever." Peregrine, who had never heard such words before, was nonetheless extremely moved, and, not knowing what to do, raised Julianus up and embraced him.

"Now, there seems to be a novel and an interesting philosophy in those phrases," said Volumnius. "In these days of crumbling empire and divided faith one does seem to feel the need of something more to cling to, even if it is only another man's knees . . ."

All the city was quiet as they emerged. There had been, of course, another way out—Peregrine had somehow known that there must be. They had frighted a great rat, as they peered and poked about there under the ground, and, by the familiar old trick of following it (familiar old tricks have generally become familiar and old because they so often work) as it darted into a particularly large pile of bones, they had found that other way. And then it was, inexplicably to his companions, that Peregrine said that he would turn back.

"Tut-tut," said Volumnius. "This is surely carrying gamesmanship too far."

"No, lord, no," said Julianus, kneeling once again, this time in supplication.

The sight of him seemed to awaken something in Peregrine's mind. "Indeed, it was not for love of the dungeon crypt that I wanted to go back," he explained, "In fact, that would be doing it the hard way. Julianus, though I know you not, one thing about you is certain, for it was that one thing which brought us both so close to death. Tell me how I may find my way to her—more safely than before, I need not say—if such is possible."

It was clear that Julianus felt his vow or pledge or oath as well as that same grateful inclination of the heart which had produced it, required that he go with Peregrine. But his terror at the thought of once more falling into the hands of Sulla was too great. "Only tell me," said Peregrine. "Is there such a way?"

Julianus considered, there in the quiet street, whilst all the city slept. Then, slowly, his bowed head came up, and he nodded. "Openly, there is no way where for

sure he may not find his way. But . . . between the
walls . . . Yes. There is a way . . .''

And so it was that Peregrine found his way, and
through deeper darkness at first than that of the crypt,
with a wall brushing him on either hand and pressing
close. And after many a turning he saw a glimmer of
light. And, measuring his breaths and his heartbeats, he
came to a halt. And pressed his eye to the chink in the
wall.

There she was, sitting upright in her chair, a lamp on
her desk, and her tablets open in her lap. "What place
did Austin mention?" she asked. And answered herself, "He did indeed mention many places. He spoke of
the sea more than once. *Thalassa, thalassa,* he would
say. He mentioned Rome and Ravenna and Byzantium.
He spoke of the great forests. And, to be sure, he
mentioned the desert and the pyramidal treasure-houses
of the Ptolemies . . . but, too, he spoke regretfully of
the great heats and thirsts of the deserts as travellers
have told.''

Peregrine raised his hand to tap gently. But that inch
or so between upraised hand and wall, his hand never
travelled. For, as though coming from almost directly
beneath it, a voice spoke, familiar and unfamiliar, slow
and dreamy and deep. "Now, easier might this one sib
of his find his own way through the trackless maze of
the great northern forests, and up from the bottom of the
deep, black sea, and across deserts with their heats and
thirsts as travellers have told, than ever he shall find his
way up and out from where he now lies and is lodged.''

"In a way it is too bad," she said. "It is too bad in a
way. For he did nothing, you know. Some absurd
scruple concerning his brother prevented him, I think.''

A wordless sound of quiet rage and smothering hate
came from the man sitting against the wall. "No scruple, absurd or otherwise, concerning me, did in any

way prevent his brother—*enough!* This one has by
virtue of his blood endorsed that other one's note: and
now payment is demanded. And pay he shall. For,
whilst it is true that the other's guilt did in no wise
exceed yours, still and still and still, you are my wife
whom I love and must forgive: and they others must I
neither. Therefore, he must suffer, he shall and he will.
—Eh? As others have before him? Yes, and, I fear, as
others shall, after him. Thus it is and will be, as long as
you are you and I am I.

There was the sound of a chair scraping. "But I
waste time, for even now I feel my rage growing hot
and strong within me. If not by the rack, then by other
means. And you must come with me, and watch, and
see what you have brought about."

Clothilda sighed and Clothilda nodded and Clothilda
arose. "If it be so, then so be it. I cannot in either event
either prevent or help. And if I, by looking on, shall
suffer, well, let it be my punishment. For though not
faithful, I am loyal. In my way I love you very much."

He took up the lamp, she took his hand, arm in arm
they went out. Peregrine, feeling rather sick, followed
by his own way. The lamp flickered like a fire-fly, the
gardens were cool. It still lacked some hours till day.
He flitted behind them on his toes and over the damp
and springy turf, from hedge to hedge. The thick door
to the crypt gave some trouble, as—he now recalled, it
had the first time—but then there had been several men
to strain. At length, however, Sulla and his lady wife
had it open. And Peregrine heard him say, "Let this
piece of wood serve as shim to keep it open until we
return, for by then I shall be weakened. It is always
so . . ."

And she murmured something sympathetic. And the
dim light dwindled, and was gone.

There was, there had been no doubt in Peregrine's

mind as to what he was going to do. He waited just what he considered long enough. Then he took up the shim. Its wood was soft, and splintered easily. He broke off some splinters of it and shoved them into the keyhole, jamming them with his hand. Then he leaned against the door until he heard the dull heavy click. Stay there, forever, of course, they would not; much though he would have wished it so. Sooner or later, if the couple did not discover the other way out, some household staff would bethink them of the crypt. Their laird's ways surely could not be unknown to all of those who served him. But, and until then—

Turning swiftly, his hands fixed in such wise as to grasp and throw whoever might lurk behind, he recognized a faint but paunchy figure. "Excuse me, sir," said a familiar voice, "but are you not the young man whom we not long ago left securely, or so we thought, shackled in the dungeon crypt?"

"And if I am, what then . . . Sempronius?"

"It is very civil of you, sir, to remember my name. Many a person in your then position might have never even noticed it; but, then, I always say, Breeding is breeding, and that's what counts. Being of breeding, then, sir, you would not wish to hold against me any actions at which I was obliged to assist on my master's orders. And of course a sorcerer of great skill, which it is hardly needful to acknowledge you must be in order to have escaped, wouldn't be bothering—may I not say 'Your Honor'?—wouldn't be bothering to afflict an enchantment upon me—"

"Stop babbling and spit it out."

Sempronius coughed again. "The *it* of it, sir and Your Honor, is that I perceive that where my master now is, is a very good place for him to is—that is, I mean, to be. And it was in my mind, in a manner of speaking, that it might be that some good friend to

Caesar might choose this moment to ask of Caesar the grant and escheat and forfeit of this villa, messuages, tenements, lands, domains, demesnes, and so forth and so on. In which case the new owner might not be averse to engaging me as his man of business as it were, his Chief Steward. Being acquainted as I am with the entire establishment, inside out as one might say, and the characters of all its personnel—''

''Knowing which thralls' fingers to dip in the boiling oil, you mean?''

Sempronius gave another splendidly noncommittal couch. ''Well,'' said Peregrine, thoughtfully, ''I shall think about it . . . . By the way, was it not the fact that when any Vestal Virgin was convicted of inchastity and inmured alive that she was said to have the choice of starving to death by lamplight, or of drinking the oil and thus surviving a little longer in the darkness?''

''A man of my own severely limited education, sir, can only marvel at the extent of Your Honor's simply superb education,'' said Sempronius.

\* \* \* \*

Darlangius Caesar Augustus was aghast. ''Why that slimy son-of-a-bitch,'' he said. ''Imagine the gall of the man, trying to imprison, torture, mutilate, and destroy my friends, in that order. Cuckoldry-shmuckoldry, what's the matter: my friends aren't good enough for him? Well, let him blanch down there like an endive. His estates are forfeited to The Purple, make a note of that, honey,'' he murmured to his secretary. ''I said, *Make* a note, not *Gouge* a note; do you think that goddamned stylus is for cutting cuticles? If you didn't have the sweetest little ass in Trans-panonia, I'd, uh, mmm,'' and his voice fell away as, with one hand he caressed the sweetest little et cetera

and with the other groped for his desk-copy of Volume
One of *The Sermons of Saint Ephraim the Deacon*.
Then, something occurring to him, he said, "Drat, I
can't do both of these and talk to you at the same time."
Laying down the patristic sermons, he cleared his
throat, and began to address Peregrine.

"The forfeited estate—And file that under:
*Forfeitures: Torture, Illegal, Abuse of;* and not under
*Escheated Estates of Intestate Bastards*—er, ah,
mumph, no offense, mboy—would be a nice little nest
egg on which to start life anew," said Caesar. "I mean.
Look here. I adopt you. Endow you with said estates.
Make you my right-hand man and Co-Heir. That makes
you the Caesar to Caesar's Caesar. Or— Anyway.
Sooner or later, all these two-drachman little caesarates
are bound to fall like ripe medlars into the ripe, I mean
right hands. Now I. Mboy. Am a man of vision. But.
Of action? No. Mean to say. Tomorrow I may get
deeply interested in codifying the agricultural laws.
The next day, however, might find me reforming the
rules for inspecting whorehouses. Demands a great
amount of empiric research, project like that. Who
—meanwhile—carries on with the *Three asses shall
hereinafter he deemed to equal one ox—?* and so on.
Not, you bet your ass, your putative adoptive Pappa,
Domitian Antonius Nerva Ahenobarbus Julius Darlangius Augustus Tiberius Theophrastus Bombastus Phil-
lipus Aureolus, um, er, ah, where in the Hell is that
note I made of whatever the Hell my entire title is? . . .
Never mind . . . You do see what I mean, my boy? I
can't even keep my hands on my own name." Considering just what he *was* keeping his own hands on at the
moment, this was perhaps not surprising.

Peregrine said, sincerely, "Caesar, I am moved by
what you say. But I am not now the man for that.
Putting pride aside, and speaking as simply and plainly

to you as I would to my own and natural father, I say this: I am really not yet a man. I am still a boy who is still in the process of passing into manhood. Who would be the man you want, is Austin.''

Caesar was himself sufficiently moved to move his hands off his secretary and to place them on his young friend's shoulders. ''Comparisons would be odious,'' he said, ''and so I am not going to make them. The point at issue is that Austin is not here and that you are.''

''You sum everything up in those words. *Austin is not here*. And because Austin is not here, therefore I can not remain here, either. When I left my father's court—and I left it, let us not forget, under a ban of death should I return armed or at the head of an armed host—all I wanted was to see more of the world. To see all that there was to be seen, was my thought. When I first had a hint of Austin's having passed by a certain way which I was also passing by, of course I wanted to see him, meet with him, be with him, too. But now I find that my feeling is more intense—I want to find him, my brother, more than I want to do anything else.

''And so, though otherwise I would much be tempted to gain by adoption a crown and title which can never be mine by descent of blood, to purge that taint, as some think it, by donning purple, I can't.''

Darlangius, listening carefully, asked if that were the only reason. The younger man was briefly silent. And then said, ''I don't dislike Chiringirium. —Where would I feel at home? I don't know. If I ever find such a place, I suppose I'd settle there. I can't help right now being reminded that my name means *foreigner . . . alien . . . wanderer . . .*''

Slowly the ruler nodded. He seemed slightly older, slightly wearier. ''I shall be sorry to lose you, my young friend . . . 'Lose you'? No, I won't lose you, but I shall certainly miss you. As I miss Austin. 'Young friends last longer, when they last at all.' Who said that? Never mind. Doesn't matter. I hope you will come back, both of you. 'Foreigner, alien, wanderer'? Yes . . . Peregrine means those things. It means something else, too—''

And, the former court-philosopher, *a capella* bard, etc., of Sapodilla, having just at that moment come in, Darlangius asked, ''Appledore . . . what else does Peregrine mean?''

''It is a kind of falcon, Your Demi-imperial Highness . . . . Well, my boy. You are leaving? Then I must give you my answer. I am not going with you. Not this time. I find that I am more tired than I had realized. Adventures merely heat the blood of the young —indeed, they may well be deemed necessary for to purge it of the thick humors which the excitations of youth engender—but they have the contrary effect upon those of us whose heads have been tempered by the snows of many decades. —In short, my boy: *Bene Valetas. Nix.*''

\*   \*   \*   \*

Appledore was present when his former pupil bade farewell to Chiringirium. The archbishop was stationed downwind and, happily swinging what must have been the largest thurible in all Christendom, intoned benedictions and sang psalms, accompanied by a choir. In a litter made brave with cloth of tissue of gold, sat the Caesar himself. Appledore was actually the requisite distance from the city gate as required by law in order for him to escape indictment for uttering pagan blessings and other ceremonies ''in any place which is either public or private.'' It had been learned that the minimum distance was one-half a bowshot plus one-

half of one-half a bowshot: and this had been carefully
measured out by the Very Reverend the Protopresbyter
of Chiringirium, an old-style ecclesiast, who was an
authority on the ecclesiastical bowshot, which was not,
of course, the same as the archers' bowshot. (Caesar
had listened to all this with great patience and had then
murmured something which might, conceivably, have
been "bowshot").

Darlangius had equipped Peregrine and party with a
lavish hand—more lavish than the hand of the poor
king of Sapodilla, by far—from a list of his own
called, somewhat unsurprisingly, the Lavish List);
ranging from *Ablution, silvern-gilt vessels, for the purpose of*, 25 to *Zithern, ebony and/or other precious
woods, made of; mother-of-pearl, inlaid with*—and,
assisted by Claud, a train of the best horses and mules in
the district to carry it all.

"Has that engrosser finished those documents I—he
has. Good. Hnd 'em up, hmm, hmm, *The Senate and
the People of Rome* hmble hmble hmble, *To Have and
to Hold From This Day Forward*, hmpty hmpty
hmpty, blbbble blibble, blibble, *great* martyred min-
nesingers! I could annex Parthia with fewer words than
this!—where the Hell—oh—here—*EXEMPT FROM
SEIZURE: CAESAR*. There. That'll do it. I hope.
Here you are, mboy. Don't forget the presents for
Austin. And, should you by any chance reach the
far-off Land of Silk, Sina or Kina or whatever they call
it, remember to send me word if it's true that the women
there—*you* know! Eh? Very well. And now . . .
oecumenicism and tolerance is all very well, but leave
Us not forget Our priorities." He raised his hand and
made a sigilation over Peregrine's head, his lips meanwhile moving in a short and silent blessing.

Next, with elaborate formality, he wheeled his horse
around and had it take four paces; then, the pious

proprieties satisfied, he wheeled the horse around again
and looked on with great interest as Appledore commenced his own ceremony. It involved, of course, corn
and wine and oil and salt and water, and was concerned
with earth and air and had some reference to fire as
well. Peregrine apprehended that he was being made
free of good things, commended to the protection of
good spirits, warded against several sundry sorts of
harm: and then the ceremony simply passed beyond his
apprehension. Briefly, he was reminded of the sage's
twice prior Fetching of the Winds, and of the cry of a
sea-bird on a stormy sea . . . . But there were differences . . . there were now neither storms nor sea, only
swiftly-rushing air, and though the chant (now it rose
and now it fell) did somehow put him in mind of birds,
they were not sea-birds.

He suddenly blinked, realized that Appledore had
finished, and that the sounds he heard were those of
Caesar's party, vigorously expectorating three times
each and making horns and figs with their fingers in
order to drive away any paganical daemons which
might have been attracted. Peregrine embraced the
sage, embraced Claud, was tearfully embraced by
Philoxena, had his hands clasped by Darlangius and in
turn killed Darlangius's hands. The trumpeters blew
long blasts on their long bell-mouthed instruments, the
Archbishop of Chiringirium swung his censer, and
everybody sneezed and gave three cheers. Then the two
parties parted, and went their different ways.

Of all the beasts and gear with which he had set forth
from his native country, Peregrine now retained but one
pair of saddle bags. In it there still reposed such remnants of his father's gifting as the pod of musk and the
six measures (or whatever number) of barley-meal,
and, packed between them and wrapped in the simple
linen of country weave, there was a curious crown and

the hilt of an equally curious sword and the shattered fragments of a blade—and none of these latter and rare things had been with him from the first.

Appledore and Claud had ridden away with him at that first; Appledore he had known for all his own young life, and Claud, for that matter, more or less. Now next to him rode Julianus, about whom he knew nothing, except that he rode very close to him indeed and never seemed to take his eyes away from Peregrine, save when he scanned the scene to assure himself of his young lord's safety. Farther off, and looking exceedingly self-satisfied, was his new steward, one Sempronius. And the rest of the retinue he did not know at all, Caesar having appointed them.

The plowman followed his oxen, the birds followed the plowman, twenty servants followed Peregrine.

And Peregrine followed the road.

Already men were earning Caesar's sesterces by commencing the work of repair on that road, and some did it merrily for reason of being able to get their bread and wine by honest time and toil, and some did it sullenly and with ill grace indeed for reason of being able to get their bread and wine by time and toil alone. The thicket was being cut back some distance away from the barm of the road as a discouragement to those who were willing to spend time lurking there in hopes of getting their own (or another's) bread and wine without the need for any toil at all. The road led away from the river, and the view was of valleys, with far away a range of hills.

Presently noon came, but, so brisk and fresh the breeze that it was a noon without great heat; and no shadows streamed away from the great triple arch as they approached, or lurked round its feet like crouching dogs. And here the road divided, and became three. The captain of the guard saluted. Peregrine returned the salute, and then, by the man's unrelaxed air being informed that something had not yet been performed that had to be, glanced aside in slight perplexity to Julianus. Who, with the slightest of movements, indicated his master's other hand. "Of course," murmured Peregrine.

He handed to the captain of the guard the pole of the pennant he had born hither from the city gates, purple with the caesarial diadem in gold, and the embroidered *D*. The captain saluted once again.

"And here ends the domain and the jurisdiction of my friend," Peregrine said, to himself, yet aloud.

Respectfully, the captain of the guard pointed out that this was not altogether the case. "According to the Demarcations set forth the last time the Three Emperors met," said the officer, "The boundaries of this province extend to those high hills yonder. However, sir, this much is so: that past this point, we do not patrol. Not yet," he added.

Peregrine pondered. Then he said, "You will be able to tell me, though, where these three roads lead."

What was probably a rare enough smile briefly creased the soldier's sun-browned face. "Well does every school-boy, sir, know that all roads lead to Rome. However. This one here does indeed lead to Old Rome—and, before that, to Ravenna. And as well to the seaports whence, if one would wish, there go ships to such further places as Egypt . . . Mellita . . . Joppa—" He waved a hand, as though to indicate they both knew he could not name them all. "And this other one, here, leads to New Rome: which is to say, Byzantium, or Byzance-town. But this last one, over there . . ." He paused, and pursed his lips. "*Its* end, I do not know. Is there perhaps a third Rome, somewhere, sir?" he did not venture upon another smile, but it lay in his words.

Again Peregrine felt that strange stirring in his mind, and he groped towards his saddle-bags. Then it seemed to him that the gesture was without meaning, and another thought overcame it, *"Thalassa, thalassa,"* he murmured.

"Ah, the sir knows the Grecian tongue," the soldier said, lookingly mildly interested. "I know it not, myself, but once, years ago, I served under a centurion who did. And he told me that that means, 'The sea! The sea!' and that these were the words the Greeks of long ago exclaimed when, after a long wandering out of Persia, they saw it before them."

Two thoughts now smote Peregrine together. He remembered what was in the saddle-bag, besides the things he had recalled not long before. And he remembered something else as well. *Now, easier might this one sib of his find his way through the trackless waste of the great northern forests, and up from the bottom of the deep, black sea . . .* He gave a slight shudder. And still the captain of the guard regarded him. And then the captain of the guard spoke.

"I have served six Caesars of Chiringirium," he said. "And I hear that this new one is the best by far of all. Tomorrow they will come to offer us his bread and salt. I have no personal feelings against him. But it is now in my mind that perhaps six caesars are enough. One loyalty is ended, another has not yet begun. And in my mind, just now, has grown the thought that I might take leave of my post here, now, without dishonor."

Peregrine wondered somewhat at the man's inmost thoughts, one stranger to another. "What is your name?" he asked. "And where do you think to do?"

"My name, sir, is Serverus . . . Where does the young sir think to go?"

The offer was plain. Peregrine, looking at the man, suddenly felt that it was not unwelcome. "This yonder road, Captain Serverus . . . Might it lead, perhaps, do you think, eventually to the great northern forests?''

"Sir, it might well, for they lie in that approximate direction, as I have heard.''

Peregrine's horse began to move a trifle restlessly, and he gentled it. "And . . . Captain . . . might it lead, perhaps, so you think, eventually to a sea? And to which one?''

White lines came and went around the eyes of Serverus as he frowned in thought. "It probably would, sir, take one thing with another. Which one? I think to that same sea the Greeks cried out at—which is strange, seeing that the road heads north, though not true north, and Persia must lie to the south as well as to the east. Its name would be that Euxine Sea, which some call Black.''

Peregrine opened the saddlebag on his right side and needed not to look whither his hand groped. "If you will come with me, then, Captain Serverus . . . if you will chance the trackless forest and the equally trackless sea . . . discharge your duties at this present post, presently. The new Caesar will not, I think, grudge me yourself. —Nor, for that matter, would he grudge me a lance for my pennant . . . That one in your hand will do, I think. The banneret itself you may return when you return to discharge yourself.''

The discharge did not take long. The second in command made no objection, naturally enough, and took from Peregrine a short note explaining matters to Darlangius; and asking that Serverus's back pay be commuted into land and administered by The Purple until such time as Serverus would return . . . or . . . whatever . . .

"All carried out and in order, sir,'' said the new captain of his troop. "What is your first order, sir?''

Peregrine handed him a piece of cloth. "My own

banneret and pennant," he said. "Fasten it to the lance-pole, Captain, and carry it yourself this first mile: and perhaps many miles, indeed, further."

The rugged face of the officer folded into lines of concentration. His hands, scarred in more places than one, were deft and quick. "Our banner, sir," he said. It took the fresh wind and whipped out that all might see.

Peregrine said, "Onward, then. North, and north by east. By road, by forest, and by Sea . . . by forest and by Sea."

And another voice spoke, close, close to his ear, spoke low, but was heard nonetheless above the sound of clinking gear and horse-hooves; it was the voice of Julianus. " 'Behold the Ram of God,' " he said, his head indicating the black figure of Ammon on the white weft. " 'Behold the Ram of God, which taketh away the sins of the world . . .' "

*　*　*　*

Now and then they met upon the road a party of woodcutters, saw the occasional smoke of a charcoal burnery. And huntsmen they saw, such as seek the yellow-deer, or red. But women and children they saw not. Plane-trees and poplars were often along the road, and beyond it in the second growth of timber, springing up on the abandoned farms, were trees unfamiliar to Peregrine. He turned to his man, riding always close to him, asked, "Those words you said, Julianus, when you first saw my pennon—what do they mean to you?"

It seemed to him that his question made the man rather more uneasy than not, but his answer came without hesitation. "Lord, once, when I was younger, I served some monks in a distant cloister which contained a number of ikons of fame and virtue. There came to us once, in the dark of night, some men who were mounted. Several stayed back, in the darkness, and even the one who rode closer kept his face muffled in his cloak . . .''

''Yes,'' said Peregrine, softly. ''Yes . . . yes . . . Go on.''

The account was a short one. The rider had asked to be shown ''the Black Lady'', a request not very welcome (as it seemed) to the abbot. There was indeed an ikon, a Madonna, the abbot conceded. But he preferred to delay opening the chapel until the next day, the nocturnal prayers being said according to custom in the main church. And, further, the abbot straightly declared, the Madonna was dark merely because the resin-treated oil with which she had been painted had darkened with age. This explanation and its suggestion of delay did not please the rider.

'' 'She is our Lady, Queen of the Dark Heavens of the Night,' '' he had said, '' 'and of the Dark Earth. Lady of the Black Soil is She, and of the Black Skies and Seas. As is She, so is Her Son: and black are they, and beautiful.'

''And the abbot, trembling, yet still staunch, declared, ''What you say is not heresy alone, it is blasphemy. And,' here he went for the chapel, fumbling for the key, 'And in Her shall I take refuge from your unholy words, Let me hear no more of that. Let your veneration be silent and brief.' '' He had thrown open the doors, gone to the ikonostasis, removed the image and held it up, murmuring prayers. And all the riders had bowed low upon their mounts, and had said their own prayers, also low.

''Then,'' said Julianus, ''They galloped away, to our old abbot's great relief and to those of his monks —and, I admit—to mine as well. But as they went, one I saw who carried a pennon on a lance, and if it was not the very one which Captain Serverus carries now, then it was its model: and certain it is that I heard him say as he flourished it and before the darkness swallowed him, those words which came to my mind and to my mouth as I saw this pennon which is now ours. —Now, my lord, this is but all I know; and if in relating it I have given any offense, for this I am heartily sorry, and forgiveness I do beg and crave for it.''

"There being no offense, there is no need for a forgiveness.''

Sempronius, who had been riding somewhat nearer than usual, seeing now that the conversation was at an end, approached. "If it please Your Honor," he said, "if I am to serve your Honor's supper as it should be served, I must be able to see to it that the cook-fires are lighted in time for good beds of coals to build." Peregrine had not been particularly keen on having Sempronius along, but Darlangius had urged him to do so. Peregrine would be riding in high estate, said Caesar, and would find his way eased accordingly: he would, as part of this estate and ease, be receiving entertainments—therefore he would have to return them.

"He's a fat futz," said Caesar, definitively, "But he knows how to handle these things, and, after all, you don't have to snuggle, cuddle, or bundle with him. If the soup isn't entirely to your liking, throw it at him. He'll like *that*. Shows him he's doing for a real gentleman. There are no snobs like servant snobs.''

The troop pitched camp. Serverus set up a perimeter of defense, Sempronius had his cook-fires started and, whilst they were still too high for cooking over, Julianus heated his master's bath water. Peregrine was bathed and anointed and changed his clothes. A small tray of thirsteners was served, then warm water was mixed with wine and poured for him. He sat on a camp chair in front of his tent and sipped from the goblet and marvelled at how things had come to pass, how changed his fortunes. Lamps were presently lit, supper was served, and served splendidly. Peregrine walked about a bit afterwards, then he retired and read in the Histories of Herodotus. Vaguely he was aware of laying the scroll aside, of Julianus first covering him with soft blankets, then blowing out the lamps and snuffing the glowing wicks with moistened fingers, and—more vaguely yet—of Julianus composing himself at the foot of his camp-bed. And then he fell asleep. And slept soundly.

Thus did day follow day and night follow night.

The road went ever on and on, and, league by league and day by day, the grassy verges crept closer to the center. Nights and days alike grew cooler, and fires were kindled for more than cooking purposes, now; and the winds blew more briskly. Trousers, which would, even in the provincial cities, have been scorned as the mark of the barbarian tribes, one day made their appearance; and were gratefully accepted and as gratefully worn.

"Quite some number of others have been round about here not long ago, Sir," Captain Serverus observed one day.

"What sort of others, then?"

"Huntsmen, I should say, Sir. Seemed to have flushed bigger game than yellow-deer or red. But that's to be expected as we get farther north and farther in towards the wilder land."

Peregrine nodded. "Well, Captain, I know you will continue to keep your eyes open, and me informed. I should like to speak with them, if our paths cross."

Travel by land since leaving Chiringirium had certainly been quieter than travel by land or by river before then. It had given him time to "settle back into himself,'' as he thought of it . . . and, thinking so, realized that the *himself* was no longer the same one as before. That night they encamped on a bare knoll which brought from Captain Serverus grunts of satisfaction, it being evidently to his way of thought ideally suited for military purposes; though such might not be Peregrine's or anyone else's purposes, the captain was what he was and what he had been trained to be. ''From here there is good view and sight,'' he said.

There was. And Peregrine, after the evening meal, walking about as usual, remarking on the fading sun and wondering if more of the same lay ahead on the marrow—feeling rather bored with the thought —regarding the view, observed a number of fires in the distance. Quite suddenly he felt that even the company and conversation of charcoal-burners, could he understand it, would be a welcome change from the sanctimonius unctuousness of his steward, the over-close and somewhat doglike devotion of his body-servant, and the crisp and impersonal attentions of his captain.

They were all at meat.

Quietly and matter-of-factly, he went to where the horses were tethered, selected a riding-horse he had not ridden that day, saddled him, and—with a word or two to the guard circling the camp on his rounds—walked the animal off. What were probably the last, late frogs of the season croaked dismally in the ditches their melancholy and unanswerable question of *Wee*-dit? *Wee*-dit? . . . or, at least, so it sounded to him. It did not sound to him at all like *brekekekex koax koax* . . . until at length, still unanswered, the question was pounded out by the sound of the quickening hooves.

He could nowhere see the fires from the level ground along the road. Several times he essayed to climb again and scout about. It was while he and his mount were

standing stick-stock-still that he observed in the dimlight a hand take hold of his bridle, heard a voice ask,
"*Quo vadis, peregrinatus?*"

The voice was neither friendly nor hostile. It took a
moment for him to realize that it had named, not his
given name, but his state of wandering. He was considering how to frame his answer, when his sword was
swiftly slipped from its scabbard.

"There was no need for that," he said, feeling,
rather than seeing the more than a few men surrounding
him . . . them . . .

The reply was not in words. The horse was led
forward into the darkness; and Peregrine, on the horse.

Branches whipped his face, and he crouched against
the neck of his mount, not looking up until the same
voice (silent throughout this going) said, "Down." He
dismounted.

Low were the fires which gave the only light, and
now and then they brightened, and now and then they
dulled. Figures, robed in color of night, crouched,
fanned the embers with their long sleeves. Other figures were clad the same. Peregrine saw no face. He
did not really realize that his hands were bound until he
tried to move them. "You who stole the banner of the
Great Black God," the voice said; "you who came to
spy: you shall stay to pray." Hands pressed against his
shoulders, hands pushed against his chest, legs prevented him from falling backward, he sank upon his
knees.

Blocks of turf were brought and piled. A black cloth
embroidered with figures and symbols which he was
unable clearly to make out, was spread over the pile.
And then once again, as in that far-off night, with Claud
and Appledore, the mystery began its enactment: this
time with two differences: he saw, as well as heard; he

was not free, but bound. The chanting, as before, was
in more than one tongue . . . in at least two . . . and,
even when it was in the one he understood, he did not
understand it all.

It was as strange to him, in its way, as the masses and
liturgies and other ceremonies which he had attended,
or, at any rate, witnessed. And it was at the same time
quite different. Darlangius had been content to ask of
him no questions, to press no points—certainly not the
point of that famous or infamous impaling-stake to
which Attila had so vividly referred—nor could Peregrine imagine Darlangius treating anyone else in such
fashion. The ceremony he was now witnessing was in
some few places now and then reminiscent of the
others; in more places it put him in mind of certain
strictly pagan ceremonies he had himself observed back
in Sapodilla. In addition, there were nuances which
were familiar (no . . . too strong a word . . .),
nuances with which he was not totally unfamiliar,
either from having read or having heard of certain
things.

*They know who I am,* was his astonished and recurrent thought. He realized that of course they need not,
probably did not, know who he was in the entirety of
*who:* did they indeed know that he was Peregrine the
son of Paladrine, by-blow to a minor king, that he had
at the age of twelve lost his virginity to the nurse-maid
of his infant half-brother, that he loved lamb dressed
with garlic and was somewhat afraid of spiders? Not
likely. Clearly, though, they knew that he, whoever *he*
was, had that pennon which—and then he tried to call
to mind all the circumstances of his having picked it
up—and then he was carried away by the unfolding
mystery. Some of the words, phrases, he had heard
before. Others were new to him.

*The great black goat . . . the ram and goat are one . . . Ammon Immanuel . . . Ammon Dulkarnahyeen . . . Essus Chresthus niger est sed formosus . . .*

"Behold the Ram of God," the chant suddenly became quite clear, "*who taketh away the sins of the world!*" But as to what he was to behold, Peregrine in the leaping darkness and the falling light, was less than uncertain. And then began a litany. "*Seventh Son of the Seventh-Born Son of God,*" a voice intoned; and, from the shadows: "*–pray for us!*"

"*Twelve Apostles of the Great Black Christ–*"

"*—pray for us!*"

"*Saint Aries–*"

"*—pray for us!*"

Caught between astonishment and confusion, Peregrine said, half-aloud, half to himself, "But Aries is itself The Ram . . ." Regardless, the litany swept on, waves advancing, breaking, ebbing, falling away:

"*Saint Taurus–*"

"Pray for us!"

"*Saint Gemini–*"

"*Saint Cancer . . . Saint Leo . . . Saint Virgo . . . Saint Libra . . . Saint Scorpio . . .*"

"Pray for us! Pray for us! Pray for us! Pray for us! Pray for us!"

In astonishment, in wonder, in confusion, in an amazement which yet acknowledged a certain logic in the invocations, Peregrine, on his knees, heard the hooded congregation continue to call upon the gods of the ancientmost heavens in the guise of apostles and saints—apostles and saints of a Christ certainly not the Christ elevated (and not so long ago) to the status of One, True and Only throughout the already crumbling remnants of the Roman Empire.

As though they were somehow not part of him he felt

his knees feeling the small rocks and twigs pressing into them. Then, suddenly, all the strange congregation rose; and he, perforce, rose with them.

"*O heavenly Ram, which leadeth the flock of the Stars . . . O Fleece of Pure Gold . . . O Ram caught in the thicket . . . goat without horns . . .*" Some phrases, unintelligible to him . . . a perceptible change in the rhythm and the tenor of the prayers . . . a pause . . .

He felt himself moving forward, forward towards that strange, strange, dark, dark altar—and then the phrase which burst in his mind as a dry tree may suddenly burst into flames, scattering sparks—

"*Take the red knife–*
"*And cut the red bread!*"

Swiftly, urgently, they brought him forward. He did not know if he were merely to witness, or, if so, what it was which he was to witness. He did not know if he was to participate, and, if so, in which way he was to participate. He knew only that he was filled with a terror, now, greater than any terror which he had ever felt before in all his life. His heart swelled, his flesh went cold, his mouth opened upon a wordless cry of fear, a cry for help. He heard the wind rushing in his ears, he heard the sound of some bird crying aloud and aloft on and in the wind. He heard the voices of many men crying aloud their own alarm and something more. He felt his bonds slipping, falling away, he felt them no more. He saw the ground and the altar and the hooded figures and the fire all falling away with incredible swiftness.

Fear gave place to an exultation which preceded even understanding. He shrieked his defiance into the wind and the night. The wind took him and he took the wind. Below him, the shrouded earth. Above him the brilliant stars. No boundaries, no borders, the limitations of no road, now held him.

The peregrine falcon sounded once more its call and its cry. It circled once, twice . . . a third time.

And then sped away, free, into the limitless night, and all the untrammeled realms of air.